To
Wills & Martha,

With much love
from

Grandma & Grandad.
x   x

The Secret of the
Lost Necklace
and Other Stories

Enid Blyton

The Secret of the
Lost Necklace
and Other Stories

Illustrated by Val Biro

AWARD PUBLICATIONS LIMITED

For further information on Enid Blyton please visit *www.blyton.com*

ISBN 978-1-84135-587-0

Illustrations copyright © Award Publications Limited

The Adventure of the Secret Necklace first published 1954
Mischief at St Rollo's first published 1947
The Children of Kidillin first published 1940
This edition first published by Award Publications Limited 2008

Published by Award Publications Limited,
The Old Riding School, The Welbeck Estate,
Worksop, Nottinghamshire, S80 3LR

10 2

Printed in Slovakia

CONTENTS

THE SECRET OF
THE LOST NECKLACE

1

An Exciting Letter

"Breakfast! Hurry up!" A loud call came from downstairs, and there was a scurry and a yell from upstairs.

"Bob! Breakfast time! Can you do my dress up at the back for me? Quick!"

Bob went to his twin sister, Mary. "Why do girls have dresses that do up at the back?" he grumbled.

"Please, Bob," said Mary. "Hurry, we'll be late!"

Bob hurried, and the dress was fastened neatly. Then both children raced downstairs and into the breakfast-room. Their father was just about to sit down.

"Ha! It's you, is it?" he said. "I had a feeling it was an elephant or two crashing down the stairs. You're just in time."

The twins kissed their mother and father and sat down to their breakfast. Mary's sharp eyes caught sight of a letter on her mother's plate.

"You've got a letter," she said, "and I know who it's from. It's from Granny, isn't it? I always know her big, spidery writing. Open it quickly, Mummy.

Perhaps she's coming to stay with us."

Mother opened the letter and read it. "No – she's not coming to stay," she said. "But she wants you to go! Would you like to?"

"Oh yes!" said both twins together. They had only once been to stay with Granny, when they were very tiny, because she lived rather a long way away, but they remembered her old, old house with its strange corners and windows.

"When can we go?" asked Bob. "As soon as we break up? I'd like to see Granny again. She's strict, isn't she – but she's kind too. I like her."

"I love her," said Mary. "I love her twinkly eyes, and her pretty white hair – and I don't mind her being strict a bit, so long as I know what she's strict about. I mean, she tells us what she doesn't like us to do, so we know. Can we go soon?"

"Granny says as soon as school ends you may go to her," said Mother, reading the letter again. "And one of the reasons she wants you is that she will have another child staying there and she thinks it would be very nice for him to have your company – somebody to play with."

"Oh," said Bob, not quite so pleased. "I thought we would be having Granny to ourselves. Who's the other boy?"

"Your cousin Ralph – you've never seen him,"

said Mother. "Your granny is his granny too, because his daddy is brother to your daddy, and Granny is their mother."

The twins worked this out. "Oh yes," said Mary. "We've never seen Ralph. Why haven't we?"

"Only because your Uncle John, his daddy, has had to travel about all over the place, taking his wife and child with him," said Father, looking up from his paper. "Very bad for the boy – no permanent schooling, no permanent home. You two will be good for him."

The twins didn't feel as if they wanted to be "good for him". It made them sound like medicine or stewed apples or prunes – things that were always "good for you".

"How old is Ralph?" asked Bob, hoping he wouldn't be much older than he was.

"Let me see – you're seven and Ralph is almost a year older – he'll be about eight," said Mother. "I've no idea what he's like, because your uncle and aunt have been out of the country for two years now, and they never send any photographs. I expect he will enjoy having two cousins to play with."

The twins got on with their breakfast. They weren't quite sure about Ralph but when they began to think about Granny, and her old house, and the big garden with its fruit trees and flowers, they smiled secretly at one another.

"Lovely!" thought Mary. "It's fun to go and stay in a new place."

"Great!" thought Bob. "I wonder if that little pony is still at Granny's – we were too little to ride him last time but this time we could. And I hope Jiminy the dog is still there. I liked old Jiminy."

There was only one more week of school to go. When the last day came, the twins raced home. "Mummy! Where are you? We've got some good news!"

"What is it?" said Mother, looking up from her mending.

"We're top of our class – both top together, Bob and I!" shouted Mary. "Isn't that a surprise?"

"Well, you've worked hard," said Mother, simply delighted. "I really am proud of you. Dear me, to think I am one of the lucky mothers whose children work hard enough to be top!"

Father was pleased too. "I shall give you each ten pounds," he said. "You can take it to spend when you are away at Granny's."

Ten pounds! What a lot of money that seemed! Bob and Mary at once thought of ice creams by the dozen, bars of chocolate, toffees and books and new crayons.

"Only two days more and we go to Granny's." said Bob, putting his money carefully into a little leather wallet. "We're lucky – top of our form – ten pounds each – and a lovely holiday at Granny's!"

Only two days more – and away they would go!

2

All the Way to Granny's

The twins helped their mother to pack their clothes in two suitcases. "It's a good thing it's summertime," said Mother. "Your things take up so little room when they are just cotton dresses and shorts and shirts."

"Don't put in any jerseys and raincoats," begged Mary. "We shan't need those!"

Mummy laughed. "What a thing to say! What would Granny think of me if the weather turned cold or wet, and you hadn't a single jersey or raincoat to wear? Don't be silly, Mary!"

Bob knew why Mary had said that. The weather was so lovely just then, the sky so blue, the sun so hot that it seemed quite impossible to think of cold or rain.

"Holiday weather!" he said. "You won't miss us too much, will you, Mummy?"

"Not if you are happy and having a good time," said Mother. "I'll be glad for you, you see. It will be strange without you, of course – but Granny's sweet and kind, and she will look after you well for

14

me. Now — where did I put those sandals?"

"Here they are," said Bob. "Have we got to keep very, very clean at Granny's, Mummy? Cleaner than at home?"

"Well, Granny has always said that your daddy was just about the dirtiest little boy she ever knew," said Mother, smiling. "So I don't expect she'll mind if you do get a bit dirty sometimes."

"Goodness, was Daddy really a dirty little boy?" said Mary in astonishment, thinking of her big, clean, nice-smelling father, with his polished shoes and well-scrubbed hands. "Bob — maybe one day you'll be as clean as Daddy!"

"There — that's really everything, I think," said Mother, shutting down the lid. "Now, what's the time? We've got just half an hour to label the suitcases and get you ready. I'm going to take you and your luggage to the station in the car."

The twins got themselves ready, and then went to say goodbye to their rooms and all the things in them. Mother had packed Bob's monkey, which he couldn't bear to leave behind, and Mary's third-best doll, Elizabeth.

"Although she's only my third-best, I love her most of all," Mary said. "She's cuddly, and she's got a nice smile, and she goes to sleep beautifully. Please pack her very carefully, Mummy."

At last they were on the way to the station. Mother bought the tickets and there they were, standing on the platform waiting for the train to rumble loudly into the station.

It came at last, whistling shrilly, making Mary jump. Mother put them into a carriage. "I'll tell the guard to come and have a look at you now and then," she said. "You'll be quite all right, because you don't have to change anywhere. Eat your sandwiches when you see a clock at some station pointing to half past twelve."

"Goodbye, Mummy!" cried both children, hugging their mother and feeling suddenly that they didn't want to leave her behind. "We'll write to you."

"Bob, you'll remember that brothers always have to take care of their sisters, won't you?" said Mother. "So look after Mary. Goodbye, dears, have a lovely time!"

The guard whistled and waved his green flag. The train grunted and went off again, pulling the carriages in a rumbling row. The twins leaned out of the window and waved wildly. When at last they could see the platform no longer they sat back in the carriage.

"It's awfully grown-up, going on a long journey by ourselves like this," said Mary. "I hope half past

twelve won't be a long time coming. I feel hungry already."

"Goodness! It's not half past ten yet," said Bob. "You can have some chocolate at eleven. Mummy gave us a bar each. What shall we do now? Look out of the window or read our books?"

"Oh, look out of the window!" said Mary. "Let's have half an hour at that, then eat our chocolate, then have a game of seeing who can count the most houses out of the window. Then we'll watch for a station clock to tell us if it's lunch-time."

The time flew by. Soon they were having their lunch, and how hungry they were. Mother had packed up some ham sandwiches, cheese and tomato sandwiches, big pieces of fruit cake, a banana each, and another two bars of chocolate. They ate every single thing.

The guard came along every now and again and chatted to them. He said he would be sure to tell them when they arrived at the right station.

"We'll know all right," said Bob, rather grandly. "We'll be looking out ourselves."

But, you know, they weren't! They both fell fast asleep after their lunch, and didn't wake up till the guard came along, shouting, "Curlington Junction! Curlington!"

He put his head in at their window. "Hey! You

there! Wake up, and get out quickly! I've got a porter for your luggage, and he's taking the cases out of my van."

Goodness! The twins almost fell out of the carriage in their hurry – and there, not far away, standing on the platform anxiously looking for them, was Granny!

She saw them at once and ran to them, hugging them both at once.

"Bob! Mary! Here you are at last, darlings! I've been so looking forward to seeing you. Come along – I've got the pony-trap outside, waiting. We'll soon be home."

Out of the station they went – and there, in the little cart, was the pony they used to know. What a lovely beginning to a holiday!

3

Cousin Ralph

The porter brought out the two suitcases that the children had with them, and stowed them in the pony-cart. Bob and Mary went to pet the small chestnut pony.

"Hello, Benny! Do you remember us?" asked Bob. "You're fatter, Benny! Mary, he remembers us!"

"Of course he does," said Granny, getting into the little pony-cart and sitting down. "He hopes you are old enough to have a ride on him this time. Ralph rides him quite a lot."

"Where is Ralph?" asked Mary, climbing into the little cart too. "Why didn't he come with you to meet us, Granny?"

"I told him to," said Granny, "but when I was ready to start he was nowhere to be seen. He's probably stalking Indians or looking for spies, or ambushing bandits."

"Oh," said Mary. This sounded rather good. The twins liked playing at cowboys and Indians themselves!

"Is Ralph nice?" Mary asked Granny.

"Well, now, I wouldn't tell you he wasn't, would I?" said Granny, cracking her whip a little to make Benny go a little faster. "You wait and see. You're all my grandchildren, and I'm fond of every one of you. Get up, there, Benny, you're very slow today! Surely you don't mind two or three in the cart and two suitcases!" Benny trotted on, flinging his head into the air every now and again. His little hooves made a merry clip-clopping noise. The children felt very happy.

"I do like the beginnings of things," said Mary, suddenly. "The beginnings of a holiday – the beginnings of a pantomime – the beginnings of a picnic. I wish beginnings lasted longer."

"They'd be middles then!" said Bob. "Granny, will it be teatime when we get home with you? I feel as if it might be."

Granny laughed. "Oh yes, it will be teatime – with new bread and my own strawberry jam – and honey from my own bees – and a chocolate sponge cake made by Cookie – you remember her, don't you? And some of those chocolate biscuits you like so much."

"Oh! Fancy your remembering that we like chocolate biscuits!" said Mary, pleased. "You really are a proper granny."

That made Granny laugh again. "Oh, I'm a proper granny all right, so just mind your P's and Q's!" she said, with a twinkle in her eye. "Now – here we are. Welcome to Tall Chimneys!"

That was the strange name of Granny's old house, and it suited it very well, because its chimneys were very tall indeed – old, old chimneys made of red brick like the house itself.

"I like your house, Granny," said Mary. "It looks old and friendly and – well, rather mysterious too. As if it had quite a lot of secrets."

"It probably has," said Granny, getting down. "It's a few hundred years old, you know. Now here comes Mr Turner to take the suitcases. We'll go in."

"Hello, Mr Turner!" called Bob. "I remember you! And oh – here's Jiminy! Jiminy, do you remember us?"

A black spaniel ran up to them, barking a welcome. The children fell on him at once. "Jiminy! You're just the same – but you're a bit fatter too! Your tongue's just as licky. Granny, he's licked my face all over."

"Then I suppose you won't think it needs washing, but it does!" said Granny. "Take the cases up to the corner bedroom, Mr Turner, and then take Benny to the stables. I shan't want him any more today."

Turner, big and strong, lifted the two suitcases easily, and ran up the stairs with them. The children went indoors, with Jiminy leaping round them in delight.

"Do you know the way up to your room?" asked Granny. "You remember? Very well, go up now, and just wash your faces and hands. You'll find a comb there for your hair."

The twins ran quickly up the big, curving staircase. They remembered the little corner

bedroom with its slanting ceiling – lovely!

"Here it is," said Bob, running in. Then he stopped suddenly. A loud, fierce voice sounded from somewhere nearby.

"Spies! I know you! Put your hands up or I'll shoot!"

There was a loud bang as if a shot had gone off. Mary gave a scream and clung to Bob. Then the door of a cupboard was flung open and out stalked a big boy, dressed in cowboy things. He grinned at them.

"Did I scare you? I hope I did! I'm Ralph!"

The twins stared at him. "What was that bang?" said Mary, her heart still beating fast.

"A paper bag! I blew it up and popped it to make you think it was a shot!" said Ralph, grinning. "I'm glad you've come. It's awfully dull here. You look rather small, though – only just little kids. That's a pity."

"We're seven," said Bob, "so we're not little kids. You're not much older yourself, anyway."

"I'm bigger, though – much bigger," said Ralph. And indeed he was. He grinned and stamped out of the room. The twins looked at each other.

Were they going to like him – or weren't they? They felt very doubtful indeed!

4

At Granny's

The twins washed their hands and went down to tea. As Granny had said, it was a very fine tea. Bob and Mary sat down, looking at the well-spread table in delight.

Ralph came in, and sat down too. He smiled cheekily at his grandmother. "I'm sorry I wasn't about when you went," he said. "I forgot the time."

"I didn't really expect you," said Granny. "Will you please go and wash your hands and face, Ralph, and take your cowboy hat off? I've told you that before."

"I'll just take my hat off," said Ralph, and threw it on the floor. Then he reached out for the bread-and-butter.

"You heard what I said, Ralph," said Granny. "No tea unless you come properly washed and tidied. Don't let me have to find fault with you in the first few minutes your cousins are here!"

Ralph scowled. He gave the table leg a kick, got up and went out of the room. He certainly didn't like being scolded in front of his small cousins!

"Ralph is very big for his age, isn't he?" said Mary, making herself a strawberry jam sandwich. "This is lovely jam, Granny — just as nice as Mummy makes at home."

"That's good," said Granny. "Yes, Ralph is big for his age — but I expect you'll find that you know much more than he does. You can teach him a lot."

This sounded rather surprising to Bob and Mary. "Can't he read then — or do sums?" she asked.

"He only reads comics, not books," said Granny, "and that's a pity. He's not very good at sums, either — but that's not quite what I meant. Anyway, you'll soon find out. He's a good boy at heart and I'm very fond of him. He'll soon shake down and be sensible, now you've come."

Mary hoped that he would! She hadn't forgotten the fright she had had when he had yelled from the cupboard, burst the paper bag, and flung himself out suddenly into their bedroom.

Ralph came down looking clean and cheerful. He had a simply enormous tea, and had to go out and ask for more bread-and-butter and honey.

"You'll have to grow more wheat for bread, keep more cows for butter, and more bees to make honey, if you have us all staying here for long!" said Mary to Granny. That made them all laugh.

"Now, if you've finished, you can go," said Granny. "Ralph, take the twins and show them everything. They will have forgotten the way round the garden and into the farmyard."

"Right," said Ralph. "Just half a minute."

He raced upstairs, two steps at a time. He came down again in a few minutes, dressed as a Red Indian, with a magnificent tail of feathers falling from his head-dress to his feet. He really looked very grand. He had a toy axe in his belt, and had daubed his face with coloured chalk.

"Good gracious!" said Granny. "I shall never get used to your face looking like that!"

"You look fine," said Bob, wishing he had a suit like Ralph's. "Come on – let's go out. I want to see round the garden again."

Once out in the garden Ralph acted like a real Red Indian, startling Mary very much. He stalked beside a hedge, bent double, and then, at the end of it, leaped high into the air with a tremendous yell, flourishing his axe.

A scream came from the other side of the hedge, and then an angry voice:

"I've told you before not to jump at me like that, Ralph! Here I am, picking peas, and you've made me upset the whole basket. You come and pick the pods up for me!"

"No, thanks!" said Ralph, and stalked on, his eye
on Mr Turner, who had just appeared out of a shed.

Mary stopped by Cookie. "I'll pick up the pods,"
she said. "Oh goodness – Ralph has pounced on
Mr Turner now!"

There was a loud yell as Ralph leaped on Turner
– and then another as Turner, startled, swung
round and flung him off roughly. Ralph hit the
ground hard and sat up, dazed. To the twins'
amazement he began to howl.

"You hurt me! You've no right to fling me about
like that. I'll tell my grandmother!"

"So will I," said Turner, grimly, and went back
into the shed again. "Cry-baby!"

Ralph got up, took a look at the twins, who stood near by feeling ashamed of him, and then ran off round a corner.

"Well, he may be big, but he's not very brave," said Mary. "Come on, let's go round the garden alone."

So they went round it, peeping into corners they remembered, dabbling in the goldfish pond, looking up into a tree they used to climb, watching the ducks on the duck-pond. They looked for eggs in the hen-house, and all the time Jiminy came round with them, his stump of a tail wagging hard.

"Everything's lovely!" said Mary. "We'll ride Benny tomorrow, and ask Granny if we can pick some of those ripe plums for her, and climb that tree!"

"I wish Ralph wasn't staying here too," said Bob – and then he jumped. A voice came from behind nearby bush.

"I heard what you said! Mean things! You're just two silly little kids!" And out leaped Ralph, flourishing his toy axe. Oh dear – what a pity he had heard what Bob had said!

5

Before Breakfast

It was lovely to wake up the next morning and see the sun streaming in at the leaded panes of their bedroom window. The twins stared out happily. They could see a long way, over hills and fields and valleys. They could see lazy cows in the fields, and white sheep dotted about the hills.

"It's going to be a lovely day," said Mary. "Oh blow, there's Ralph!"

Ralph had the room next door. He was getting up and sounded as if he were pulling open all the drawers, moving half the furniture, and dropping dozens of things on the floor. He certainly was a very noisy boy!

He suddenly gave a tremendous rap on their door and yelled loudly:

"Come on, lazy-bones! Buck up! It's half past seven."

He then flung open the door. He was now dressed as a sailor, in long blue trousers, wide at the ankles, a blue shirt with a big sailor collar, and a sailor hat. He saluted smartly and grinned.

"However many fancy dresses have you got?" asked Mary.

Ralph stopped smiling, and gave a scowl, "They're not fancy dresses. They're the real thing, only made my own size. Fancy dresses! You don't know what you're talking about!"

He slammed the door and was gone. "Goodness!" said Mary. "What a boy! Come on, let's get up and go out. It's a heavenly day."

They were soon out in the garden. They helped Cookie to feed the hens, and then took some bread to feed the ducks. A small pebble whizzed by Bob's ankles and into the pond with a splash. He turned round.

Ralph was near by, still in his sailor suit,

laughing. He threw another pebble and it hit a duck on the back, making it scurry over the pond, quacking.

"Don't do that," said Mary, at once. That was a silly thing to say to Ralph, of course. He at once picked up a bigger stone and threw it into the pond, making the ducks swim away to the sides at once.

"Look here," said Bob, stepping right up to Ralph, who was quite a head taller than he was. "Look here, you are not to throw stones at the ducks. That's a mean thing to do – to hurt creatures that have never done you any harm."

"Pooh!" said Ralph, and bent to pick up another stone. Someone leaped on him fiercely, and he fell face downwards to the ground. He felt slaps on each side of his face and yelled loudly.

"I'll tell Granny on you, Bob! Getting me down like this! You bully! I'll tell Granny!"

He managed to get up, and glared at his attacker – and what a surprise he got! It wasn't Bob who had leaped at him and slapped him – it was Mary! A very small and angry Mary, her cheeks red, her eyes bright and hard.

"It wasn't Bob," she said. "It was me, Mary! It served you right for throwing stones at the ducks. Come along and we'll tell Granny I knocked you over and slapped you. Come on, I don't mind."

But Ralph wasn't going to tell anyone that a small girl had attacked him and slapped him, nor was he going to tell the reason why. He went very red and looked ashamed.

"I wasn't really stoning the ducks," he said. "I only meant to startle them — they're silly creatures, anyway."

"Well, I'll slap you again if you try any more tricks like that!" said Mary, who was never afraid to stick up for anything smaller or weaker than herself. "Or Bob will. You're a coward! You think yourself so big and grand, dressing up and acting like a Red Indian, or a cowboy or something — and you're really just a nasty little boy and a cry-baby!"

A bell rang out. Ralph gave a feeble smile and brushed himself down. "All right, all right, Miss Sharp-Claws. There's the breakfast bell. We'll have to go in."

Granny didn't know that anything had happened before breakfast, and nobody told her. They all ate their cornflakes and boiled eggs and bread-and-butter, and chattered away to Granny.

"I thought we would take Benny and the pony-cart and go down to the river this morning," said Granny. "We could take a picnic lunch with us — and you can paddle, if you like."

"Ooooh — let's!" said Mary, delighted. Ralph took up a spoon and banged it on the table, making Granny jump.

"Fine! Grand!" he shouted. "I'm a sailor today, and I want to get near water. Hurrah!"

"That's enough, Ralph," said Granny. "Put that spoon down. You're not a baby now!"

"We could have a swim!" said Bob. "Oh Granny, it's a lovely idea of yours!"

The twins ran off in excitement after breakfast. Where were their swimsuits? Granny had unpacked for them and put them into one of the drawers. They found them and were just going downstairs when they ran into Ralph. He looked gloomy.

"What's up?" said Bob. "Hurry, because the pony-cart is at the door already."

"I don't want to go," said Ralph. "It's a silly idea of Granny's. Let's not go."

"But you wanted to!" said Bob, in surprise. "Don't you remember how you banged the spoon on the table? Why have you changed your mind?"

Granny's voice came up the stairs. "Come along, all of you. We're just starting. Hurry up now!"

6

Ralph Gets Into Trouble

Benny the pony was ready with the little pony-cart. They all got in, and Granny put the picnic-basket down at their feet.

"I'll drive," said Ralph, who still looked rather gloomy. He picked up the whip, jerked the reins and they set off down the drive.

"Don't jerk Benny's head like that," said Granny. "There's no need to."

Benny trotted merrily out of the gate and into the lane. He slowed down when he came to the hill, and Ralph cracked the whip. Benny didn't hurry, and he flicked the little pony, making him jump.

"Give me the reins," said Granny, at once. "You pretend you've ridden so many horses, Ralph, but you don't even know how to treat a willing little pony pulling four people up a hill. Here, Mary — you drive him."

Mary took the reins and Benny felt the difference in handling at once. He went well up the hill, and then Bob had a turn. Ralph sat looking gloomy again, kicking his foot against the side of the cart.

"Cheer up, Ralph," said Granny. "You look like one of my hens left out in the rain."

That made them all laugh. Ralph cheered up and began to boast. "I've been up in an aeroplane," he said to the twins. "I bet you haven't! And I've seen the Niagara Falls crashing down like thunder. One of these days I'm going to go over those falls in a boat. I've seen real Red Indians – and chased them too. And I've . . ."

"Keep to the truth, Ralph," said Granny. "We all know you've travelled a great deal but we none of us believe that you ever chased Red Indians."

"Look – there's the river away across those fields!" said Mary, in delight. "Isn't it blue? How long will it take us to get to it, Granny?"

"About twenty minutes," said Granny. "Dear me, where is my sunshade? I didn't think the sun would be so hot. You will enjoy a paddle, my dears!"

"We've brought our swimsuits," said Bob. "Daddy taught us to swim last year. I can do breast-stroke, side-stroke and backstroke, Granny."

"Well done!" said Granny. "What can you do, Ralph?"

"Oh, I can do all those, and the crawl too. Easy!"

said Ralph. "I can swim underwater as well. I swam under longer than anyone else last year. I can life-save too."

"Well, you are big and strong," said Granny. "You should be able to life-save splendidly."

"Let's paddle first," said Mary. "Then swim. Then have our picnic. And then could we have a boat, Granny? Rowing is easy, isn't it, Ralph?"

"Oh yes!" said Ralph. "So is sailing. I sailed a great big boat all by myself last year."

"Did you really?" said Bob, impressed. "My daddy hasn't taught us sailing yet. Only rowing."

They came to the river and settled Granny in a nice shady spot under a tree. Then they all took off their shoes and socks and paddled in the cool water. It was lovely!

"Paddling's better than swimming any day!" said Ralph suddenly. "Let's not bother to swim."

"Oh, but we must!" said Mary. "I love swimming – and perhaps you could teach us the crawl, Ralph. We don't know it."

Ralph looked gloomy again, and gloomier still when Bob went to put on his swimming trunks. Then he suddenly called out: "Goodness me – I've forgotten my swimming trunks! I can't go in to swim after all – what a pity!"

"Well, look – I've brought two pairs!" said Bob,

generously. "I thought I'd wear one pair this morning and another dry pair this afternoon – but you can have them. They will be a bit small, that's all."

"Oh no, I don't want to wear yours," said Ralph – and then he heard Granny's voice.

"For goodness sake put on Bob's swimming trunks!" she called. "A swim will do you good!" So Ralph put them on, looking very cross.

They all went into the water. Ralph went in up to his waist, and stood there, shivering. Bob and Mary dived under and came up, swimming strongly and well. Granny clapped them, delighted.

"Go in, Ralph, go in!" she cried. Bob swam up behind him, dived down and caught his legs. Into the water went Ralph, right over his head. He came up spluttering and screaming:

"You'll drown me, you'll drown me!"

Bob stared at him in surprise. "Well, swim then, silly – go on! Show us how to do the crawl."

But Ralph merely stood there, shivering and looking miserable. Mary swam up to him and stood up. "I know what's the matter with you!" she said. "You can't swim, Ralph! That's why you left your trunks behind. That's why you didn't want to come. Baby!"

"You horrid girl!" cried Ralph, and tried to slap

Mary. He stumbled forward, stepped into a
suddenly deep place, and went under the water.

"Save him!" yelled Mary. "It's deep here, Bob.
Save him!"

So Bob had to life-save poor Ralph, and drag
him to shore, kicking and howling with fright.
Dear, dear, what a to-do!

"For goodness sake, let's have lunch!" said
Granny. "And if Ralph doesn't stop howling I'll try
slapping – I believe that is quite good for people
who think they have been half drowned!"

And, as you can guess, the great sailor-man was
quiet at once. How the others laughed!

7

The End of the Day

The picnic went off very well, once Ralph became sensible again. He certainly ate a great deal. Granny said she didn't know where he put it all!

"Now what about a boat?" said Granny, after the picnic. "Do you want to go rowing?"

"Oh yes," said Bob and Mary.

Granny turned to Ralph. "You said you knew all about rowing and sailing. Do you? Because I am not going to let anyone go out in a boat unless they really know about boats – especially someone who can't swim."

"Well – I don't know very much," said Ralph, going rather red.

"That's just what I thought," said Granny. "You stay here with me, then – and you, Bob, go to the boatman's cottage down there, and get his little boat for yourself and Mary."

Soon the twins were rowing back to Granny. Ralph, looking fine in his sailor-boy suit, sat and watched them sulkily. He ought to be rowing – he was dressed as a sailor, wasn't he? And yet he couldn't swim or manage even a small boat. He felt very small.

They went back home to tea, tired out, sunburnt, and the twins very happy, though Ralph was still sulky.

"Oh, I'm quite tired with all my rowing and swimming," said Mary, flinging herself down on the lawn after tea.

"Have a book, and read it quietly," said Granny.

"Oooh yes – we've brought some exciting ones away with us," said Bob, remembering. "I'll get them. They are all about seven children who make a secret society and have adventures."

He brought out three books and gave one to Ralph. "Here you are – you'll enjoy this," he said. "I'll lend it to you."

"I'd rather go and climb trees," said Ralph. But Granny wouldn't let him, so he opened the book sulkily. The other two settled into theirs and there was a silence that Granny quite enjoyed. Then suddenly Ralph shut his book.

"I've finished it," he said. "Now can I go and climb trees, Granny?"

"You can't possibly have finished it," said Granny. "You know you haven't! You can't climb trees. Sit and do nothing – or read your book properly."

"I tell you I've read it all," said Ralph. "I read quickly, not slowly like Mary there – she takes ages to turn a page!"

"Be quiet, I want to read," said Bob, and Ralph said no more. Soon Granny fell asleep and Ralph nudged Bob.

"I'm going to climb trees," he whispered. "I can't sit here and read any more."

"You haven't read a word. I don't believe you can read!" said Bob.

"I can! I can read very difficult words – and very fast too!" said Ralph. "Don't wake Granny. I'm off!"

And he crept away to where the trees grew in a little thicket at the bottom of the garden. Bob and Mary let him go. They were tired of him!

Granny woke up and looked at her watch. "Good gracious! It's time for bed and your supper. I'll bring it up to you. Where's that boy Ralph? If he has gone to climb trees I shall be very cross."

They all three went indoors. Ralph was not to be seen. And then, just as Bob and Mary were getting undressed, yells came from down the garden.

"Help! Help! Come and help me!"

Bob pulled on his shirt again and tore down the stairs, with Mary following him. They went to the bottom of the garden, where the yells came from.

Turner was there as well, grinning all over his face.

"Here's a clever boy!" he said. "Climbs trees like a monkey and then is afraid to get down! No one is going to climb up to you, so come on down!"

"Fetch a ladder!" called Ralph. "I've torn my sailor shirt already. Get me a ladder."

But Turner wouldn't – and in the end Ralph had to slither down by himself, scratching his hands, and tearing his trousers as well as his shirt. Granny was very cross with him when at last he came in.

"Go and have a bath – and tomorrow please put on a pair of shorts and a shirt," she said. "Wait till you are braver and more sensible before you parade about as a Red Indian, or a cowboy or sailor!"

Poor Ralph went to bed without any supper. He said he couldn't eat any because he felt sick, but Bob was sure it was because he couldn't bear to be scolded in front of the twins.

It was a nice supper too – stuffed eggs and jam tarts to follow. Mary was most surprised to see that Bob had taken two stuffed eggs and four jam tarts. How greedy!

But he had one of the eggs and two of the tarts for Ralph! Ralph was silly and he didn't like him, but Bob knew how horrid it was to go without supper. It is such a very long time till breakfast if you don't have supper.

Ralph was surprised and very grateful. "Oh thanks!" he said. "You are a friend. I say – it looks as if it's going to rain tonight, doesn't it? What a shame! I don't want to stay indoors all day."

"Oh, it may be fine again tomorrow," said Bob. "Goodnight – and don't dream about swimming or you'll wake up drowning!"

He went off to his room and looked out of the window. It was pouring with rain. Bother. It would be so dull staying indoors all day. But it wasn't dull. It turned out to be really very exciting!

8

Granny Sets a Few Puzzles

The next day was dark and rainy. The sun was hidden behind thick clouds, and Granny wondered what to do with the children.

"I'll set you a few puzzles," she said. "And the prize shall be a box of chocolates. Here's the first puzzle. Go into the dining-room and have a good look round. Count all the clawed feet you can see there, and come back and tell me the number. Then I'll set you a few more puzzles."

"Oh, I know four clawed feet there!" said Ralph. "The stuffed fox!"

"Don't give things away!" said Mary. They went into the dining-room and looked around. Yes – stuffed fox – and a stuffed bird with clawed feet. And a picture of an owl, he had clawed feet too.

Bob noticed a little statue of a lion on the mantelpiece – four more clawed feet. He wondered if the others would notice it.

A bell rang after a time. That was to say that their time was up and they were to come back and report to Granny. "Well," she said, when they arrived. "How many clawed feet did you see, Ralph?"

"I bet I got the most!" said Ralph. "I counted twelve – fox, owl, hawk and lion!"

"I got those twelve too," said Bob.

"I got forty-four clawed feet!" said Mary, almost crowing in delight.

"You didn't!" said Ralph. "What are they?"

"Lion, fox, owl, hawk – and the table has four clawed feet, and so have each of the chairs, and the sideboard!" said Mary.

"Right!" said Granny. "They are old chairs and table – the kind that have carved legs holding a ball in the claws of the foot. Well done, Mary."

"Jolly good!" said Bob. "What's the next puzzle, Granny?"

"Go into the drawing-room and count all the roses you can see," said Granny. So off they ran.

"Fourteen roses in that vase – and sixteen in this one – and a rose embroidered on that cushion – and another on the firescreen," thought Mary. "Any on the carpet? No. Any on the curtains? No!"

They were soon back again. "Mary, how many?" said Granny.

"Thirty-two," said Mary.

"Thirty-one," said Ralph, who had counted the ones in the vases wrongly.

"Sixty-two!" said Bob, proudly. And he was right! "I looked up at the ceiling, Granny, and it had roses carved on it," he explained. Granny nodded.

"Yes — those roses were carved long ago. You were clever to notice them. Now — one last puzzle. In the gallery upstairs there are portraits of six women who lived in the olden days — great-great-great-grandmothers of yours and mine. In five of their pictures appears the same thing. I want you to tell me what it is."

The children ran off to the gallery. It was dark up there and Bob switched on the lights. The big portraits looked down on them from the walls,

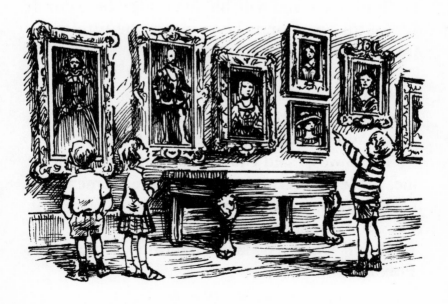

most of them dark and dingy for they were very old. There were both men and women, and the children picked out the six women and looked at them carefully.

"I know, I know!" cried Mary and ran downstairs to Granny. The two boys stared and stared at the six pictures but all the women in them wore different dresses, different collars, different cuffs. Nothing in the pictures seemed the same. They gave it up.

"What's the answer, Mary?" asked Granny when the boys joined them downstairs.

"The necklace!" said Mary. "I could hardly see it in the first two portraits – but it was quite clear in the third one – and half-hidden under the collar of the fourth one – and shone out in the fifth one – but it wasn't in the sixth picture."

"Yes. Quite right. You shall have the box of chocolates," said Granny. "Here it is."

"Granny, have you got that old necklace?" asked Mary. "Was it a kind of family necklace?"

"Yes, it was," said Granny. "It was a magnificent one, made of pearls, and each of the women who lived in this house wore it. But I can't wear it, because it disappeared about a hundred years ago."

"How?" asked Mary, handing round the chocolates.

"Well, it's supposed to be hidden somewhere in this house," said Granny. "But people have looked everywhere, as you can guess – so I fear it must have been stolen. How I should have loved to wear it! It ought to go to your own mother, after me, Mary – but it will never be found now!"

"We'll look for it!" cried Bob. "A treasure-hunt! Who's for a treasure-hunt! This very afternoon!"

"We are, we are!" shouted Mary and Ralph. Mary turned to Granny. "Granny, is there a plan of the house anywhere?"

"There may be, in one of the old books in the study," said Granny. "They haven't been opened for years, and are as dull as can be. But you might find a plan of the house if you can find a history of it – there should be one or two books about it."

So, that afternoon, three excited children went to the study and began taking down the old books there. How dusty and dull they were – and what strange printing they had!

"Here's one about Granny's house, Tall Chimneys, look!" said Bob, at last. "Now – let's see if there's a plan of the house. It might show secret passages or something. Ooooh look – there *is* a plan!"

9

The Old, Old Book

The three children bent over the old book.

It was a history of Tall Chimneys, Granny's house. At the beginning of it were some strange old maps. "This one shows the grounds," said Bob. "And this one shows the two farms. And this one – what's this one?"

They pored over the yellowed map. "It's the cellars of the house!" said Mary, pointing to an oddly-printed word. "What's the next map?"

Bob turned over the page. "This plan seems to be of the ground floor," he said. "Yes, look – this very room we are sitting in is marked – it says 'Library'. Isn't it peculiar to think that people sat in this very place, hundreds of years ago, perhaps looking at this same book!"

Mary was peering closely at the map. She had seen something strange – at least, it seemed strange to her. "Look!" she said. "There's a little door marked in the wall here – in the plan, see – but I can't see one in the real room we're in, can you?"

"Only the door we came in by – and that is marked on the plan too, in its right place," said Bob, excited. "Quick! Let's see if there is a secret door we haven't noticed in the wall over there!"

The walls had bookcases all round them. The children tried to move out the great shelves that hid the wall where a door was shown in the plan. But they couldn't. It really was terribly disappointing.

"Let's go and tell Granny," said Mary.

"No. We just might find the door somehow and, who knows, we might find a hiding-place behind it where the necklace was put for safety – perhaps during a war or something," said Bob, his face red with excitement.

Mary ran through the pages of the old book, hoping to find other maps. Two words suddenly caught her eye: 'Secret passage'! It was a wonder she saw them, because they were printed in old-fashioned letters, and the letter s was just like f! She put her finger on the words at once, afraid she would lose them.

"Look – there must be something about the secret door on this page!" she said. "I just noticed 'Secret passage'! I expect the door leads into it. Oh dear – can we possibly read this funny old printing?"

Bob read the words out slowly. "The – secret – passage was – made, er – er . . ."

Mary went on. "Was made – when – the house – was – er, was built. The door – to it – leads – er – leads from the – library. It . . ."

"Isn't this thrilling!" said Bob. They read the whole page slowly – and on it were the directions for moving the big bookcase and getting at the door!

"I say – if we follow these directions, we can get through that door and see where the secret passage goes to!" said Bob, his eyes shining. "What an adventure!"

They took the old book to the big bookcase. Mary tried to read the first direction, but it was so very dark in that corner that she couldn't. She gave the book to Ralph.

"Now you take the page over to the window and read out the directions to us one by one," she said. "That will be a help. Bob and I will do what the directions say. I remember the first one – take out the fifth book."

"Yes, but from what shelf?" said Bob. "Hey, Ralph! What shelf do we have to take the fifth book from? Buck up, silly! Can't you read what's printed there? We've read it out loud once already!"

"Er – the fifth book," repeated Ralph, his eyes on

the book. "From the – er – the ninth shelf."

"Ninth shelf. Let's count," said Mary, and they counted. "It's pretty high up," she said. "We'd better get the ladder."

So they went to the kitchen and got the little ladder. They wouldn't tell Cookie what they wanted it for, and were really very mysterious about it!

They took it to the study – and just then the tea-bell rang. How very annoying!

"Well, we'll come back at once, after tea," said Bob. "Now — not a word to Granny. We'll find out simply everything and then give her a big surprise."

So they didn't tell Granny and talked about all sorts of other things. But just now and then Bob nudged Mary and smiled at her, and she knew what he meant — "What fun we're going to have after tea!"

They went back to the study afterwards and put the ladder against the ninth shelf. Bob climbed up while Mary held the ladder. Ralph watched.

"Ninth shelf," said Bob. "Wait a minute — I must know if the fifth book has to be taken from the right of the shelf or the left. Ralph, look up the directions and see. Take the book to the window again."

Ralph pored over the page. Bob grew impatient. "Oh for goodness sake, buck up, Ralph. What does it say? Right or left?"

"Er — right," said Ralph. "Sorry. I lost the place."

In excitement Bob took the fifth book from the right of the ninth shelf. He gave it to Mary. Then he put his hand into the gap left by the book, and felt about there. What would he find? A handle? A knob to turn? A lever to pull? It was too exciting for words!

10

A Quarrel

"Can you feel anything there?" asked Mary. "Quick, tell us!"

"I can't feel a thing!" said Bob, disappointed. "Not a thing! Wait, I'll take a few more books out and see."

He handed down a few books to Mary and then felt around at the back of the shelf again. No — there was nothing there — no knob, no handle, nothing!

"You come up and try, Mary," said Bob, at last. He climbed down, his hands black with dust.

"Let's just count the shelves again to make sure we've got the ninth," said Mary. They counted — and found that they had been right before. The shelf that Bob had been looking along was certainly the ninth.

Then Mary went up the ladder and felt all along the shelf, sliding the books to and fro so that she could reach. Bob moved the ladder when she could reach no further.

"Nothing!" said Mary. "It's too disappointing for

words. Ralph, you have a turn."

Ralph went up, but, of course, he couldn't find anything either! The three children looked at one another, frowning. Now what could be done?

Mary went to the window and picked up the old book, which Ralph had put down on the broad wooden sill. She read down the page and then she gave a sudden squeal.

"It isn't the ninth shelf – it's the fifth! It says so quite clearly. And it's the fifth book we're to move, as we thought – but it's the fifth on the left, not the right, as you said, Ralph. Why did you tell us wrong?"

Ralph said nothing. He just scowled. Bob lost his temper and stamped his foot.

"You're mean! Yes, mean, mean, *mean*! You told us wrong so that we wouldn't find the secret door – and you meant to find it yourself when we weren't here."

"I didn't," said Ralph.

"You did, you did! It's just like you. You gave us wrong directions and knew we wouldn't find the door. But we shall, see. And we'll turn you out of this study and lock the door so that you won't be here to see!"

Bob gave Ralph a rough push but he stood his ground. "No, don't! I want to see the secret door. I

tell you I didn't mean to find it by myself without you. I tell you I—"

"We don't believe a word!" said Mary. "Not a single word. You boast and you tell stories and you pretend to be so big and bold but all the time you're mean — and a cry-baby too. We won't let you find the secret door with us! Go out of the room!"

"I shan't," said Ralph. "I'm bigger than either of you, and I won't go out. So there!"

Bob and Mary began to push and shove him and Ralph shoved back. They all fell over in a heap — and at that very moment Granny put her head in at the study door.

"What are you doing? Haven't you heard the bell to tell you it's bedtime? At least, it's almost bedtime, but I thought you'd like me to tell you a story first."

"You tell it to Bob and Mary, Granny," said Ralph, quickly. "I don't want to hear one tonight."

Bob glared at him. He knew quite well what was in Ralph's mind. He was going to find that secret door while he and Mary were listening to Granny! Just like him! But how could Bob stop him, unless he told Granny everything? And he did so want to keep it all a secret!

"Well, if you don't want to hear the story, Ralph,

you can go up and run the bathwater," said Granny, much to the twins' relief. "I know you like doing that. But if you let it go above halfway I shall be very cross with you. I'm not going to have the bathroom swimming in water, like last week!"

Ralph went off, frowning. Now he wouldn't be able to stay in the study on his own. Still, the others would be hearing a story, and they wouldn't be able to do any exploring either! He cheered up a little and went to turn on the taps.

He wondered if he would have time to slip down to the study while the bath was filling.

"No, I'd better not," he thought. "I might get excited and forget the bathwater – and Granny might quite well tell me off if the floor gets flooded again. But I'll be sure to keep close to the others all day tomorrow, so that they can't find that secret door without me!"

Granny told the twins a story, then kissed them and sent them up to bed. "I'll be up in a minute," she said, "and I'll bring your supper – bananas and cream. Begin to get undressed, and tell Ralph I'm just coming. He's probably sailing his boat in the bath."

He was. He wouldn't speak to the twins when they came up, and they didn't speak to him either, except to say that Granny was coming. They were soon all in bed, eating sliced bananas and cream, with sugar all over the plate – lovely!

Granny tucked them in, said goodnight and left the twins in their room. Then she went to tuck Ralph in too.

Bob began to whisper to Mary. "Mary, listen! If we leave everything till tomorrow it will be very difficult to find the door without Ralph being there and I won't let him share in this now – so what about trying to find it tonight, when Granny is in bed?"

"Oh yes!" said Mary, thrilled. "Yes, Bob! We'll keep awake till we hear Granny going to bed and then we'll creep down to the study. Oh! What an adventure."

11

In the Middle of the Night

Granny had some friends to see her that night. They stayed late, and it was difficult for the children to keep awake. In the end they took it in turns to keep awake for half an hour, sleeping soundly in between.

At last Bob, who was the one awake, heard the cars leaving at the front, and heard Granny coming upstairs. Click – click – click! That was the light switches being turned off. Now, except for a light on the landing outside, and in Granny's room, the house was in darkness.

Bob woke up Mary. "The visitors have gone," he whispered. "And Granny has come up to bed. Let's put on our slippers and dressing-gowns and go down. Granny won't hear us or see us now she's in her bedroom."

Mary leaped out of her bed, wide awake with excitement. She switched on her torch and put on her slippers and dressing-gown. "My fingers are shaking!" she whispered to Bob. "Oh Bob – isn't this exciting?"

They went down the stairs very cautiously, and came into the big hall. The moon shone in through the window there and lit up every corner. Mary was glad. She didn't like pitch-black shadows!

They went into the study. The moon shone through the windows there too, and showed them the ladder still up by the big bookcase. They went to it.

"Now – the fifth book on the fifth shelf, counting from the left," said Bob. He went up the ladder and then came down again. "I can reach the fifth shelf easily without using the ladder!" he said, and pushed it aside.

He took out the fifth book from the left of the fifth shelf and gave it to Mary. Then he began to feel about at the back of the gap where the book had stood. Mary stood watching him, trembling in excitement, trying to shine her torch where it would best help Bob.

He gave a little cry. "Mary! There's something here – a sort of knob. I'm twisting it – no, it won't twist. I'll pull it – oh, it's moved!"

There was a noise as he pulled the knob, and then another noise – a creaking, groaning noise. The bookcase suddenly seemed to push against Bob, and he stepped back, surprised.

The whole case was moving slowly out from the

wall, leaving a small space behind it, just big enough to squeeze through. The knob worked some lever that pushed the bookcase forward in a most ingenious way! Mary stared, holding her breath. How strange!

"The secret door will be behind the bookcase!" said Bob, forgetting to whisper in his excitement. "I'll squeeze behind and see if I can find it."

He squeezed himself behind, shining his torch on the wooden panelling. Mary heard him take a sudden breath. "Yes! It is here, Mary! The old, old secret door! It must be years and years since anyone went through it."

"Can you open it?" asked Mary, her voice trembling. "Oh, Bob!"

Bob was feeling all over the small door, which appeared to be cut out of the panelling. His fingers came to a little hole and he poked his first finger through it. It touched something, and there was a click as if a latch had fallen.

The door swung open suddenly and silently in front of Bob. A little dark passage was behind, and Bob shone his torch into it. "Mary! Come on! I've got the door open and it leads into the secret passage. Let's see where it goes. Come on!"

Mary squeezed herself behind the bookcase to the open door. It was no higher than her head. Bob was already in the passage, and he held out his hand to her. "Come on. It goes upwards here, in steep steps, behind the panelling. Hold my hand."

It was dark and musty in the passage, and in one or two places they had to bend their heads because the roof was so low. It seemed to be a secret way behind the panelled walls of the study – but as the steps went on and on upwards Bob guessed they must now be behind the walls of some room upstairs.

The passage suddenly turned to the left, and then instead of going upwards ran level. It came to a sudden end at another door – a sturdy one this

time, studded with big nails. It had a handle on the outside in the shape of a big iron ring, and Bob turned it.

The door opened into a tiny room, so tiny that it could only hold a wooden stool, a little wooden table, and a narrow bench on which there was an old, rotten blanket.

A wooden bowl stood on the table, and a tumbler made of thick glass. They could see nothing else inside the room at all.

"This is an old hidy-hole," said Bob, almost too excited to speak. "I wonder how many people have hidden here from their enemies, at one time or another? Look, there's even an old blanket left here by the last person."

"There's no sign of the necklace," said Mary, shining her torch round the tiny room. "But look, Bob, what's that in the wall there?"

"A cupboard — a very rough one," said Bob. "Not much more than a hole in the wall. Give me the stool, Mary. I'll stand on it and shine my torch inside!"

He stood on the stool, and peered into the hole, holding his torch to light him. He gave a cry and almost fell off the stool.

"Quick! Get up and look, Mary! Oh quick!"

12

The Hidy-Hole

Mary pushed Bob off the stool and stood on it herself, her heart beating fast in excitement. She shone her torch into the hole. At once something sparkled brilliantly, and flashed in the torchlight!

"Bob! Is it the necklace?" she cried. "Oh Bob!"

"You can be the one to take it out," said Bob. "Be careful of it now – remember it may be worth thousands of pounds!"

Half fearfully Mary put in her hand. She took hold of the sparkling mass, and gave a squeal.

"There are lots of things – not only a necklace. A bracelet and rings and brooches, oh, they're beautiful, Bob!"

"Hand them out to me one by one," said Bob. "Carefully now. Oh, Mary – whatever will Granny say?"

Mary handed Bob the things, a bracelet that shone like fire with red rubies, another one that glittered with diamonds, rings with stones of all sizes and shapes, brooches – and last of all the magnificent pearl necklace that the twins had seen

round the necks of the five women in the portraits!
Yes, there was no doubt of it, this was the long-lost
necklace!

Bob put all the jewels in his dressing-gown
pocket. It was the only place he could put them.
They felt quite heavy there!

"Now let's go and wake Granny!" he said, as
Mary got off the stool. He shone his torch on the
door, which had closed behind them. "Come on,
Mary. I wonder what Ralph will say when he
knows we've got the jewellery!"

"I don't care what he says!" said Mary. "He
didn't deserve to share in our adventure because of
his meanness in reading out the wrong directions
to us!"

Bob was trying to open the door. "It's funny –
there's no handle this side," he said. "I wonder
how it opens."

He pushed it, but it wouldn't move. He pulled it
and shook it, but it didn't open. He kicked it, but
it stayed firmly shut.

Mary suddenly felt frightened. "I say, Bob –
wouldn't it be dreadful if we couldn't get it open?
Would we have to stay here for ever?"

"Don't be so silly! Somebody would find the
bookcase was moved, and would explore and
discover the secret door, and come up the passage

and find us here," said Bob.

"But I don't want to be here all night!" wailed Mary. "I don't like it – and my torch is getting very weak. I hope yours is all right. I don't want to be here all in the dark."

"I shall look after you," said Bob, firmly. "You know that brothers always look after their sisters. Just think of all the lovely treasures we've got tonight, Mary. What about putting everything on? That will help you to pass the time."

Mary thought that was a very good idea, and soon she was gleaming brightly as she put on brooches, bracelets, rings and necklace! The rings were too large so she had to close her hands to keep them from falling off.

"You look wonderful!" said Bob, shining his torch on Mary. "Like a princess!"

Suddenly they heard a noise and Mary clutched at Bob. "What was that?" she whispered. "Did you hear it?"

The noise came again. A kind of shuffling noise – was it somebody coming up the passage? Who could it be? Surely nobody lived in this little secret room?

The twins stood absolutely still, hardly daring to breathe, and then they heard a familiar voice.

"Hey! Bob! Mary! Are you here?"

"Ralph!" yelled the twins, feeling extremely glad to hear his voice. "Yes, we're here but we can't open the door from this side. Open it from your side, will you?"

Ralph turned the handle outside and the door opened! He looked in, shining his torch. When he saw Mary, sparkling and glittering in the beam of his torch, his mouth fell open in surprise. He could hardly say a word.

"Oh!" he said at last. "So you found the necklace then! You might have waited for me, Bob."

"I like that!" said Bob. "You weren't going to wait for us, were you? You've got up in the middle of the night to come and explore all by yourself, haven't you? And you found that we were before you!"

"No. No, Bob, you're wrong," said Ralph earnestly. "I couldn't go to sleep tonight, because I was worried that you thought I was so mean. You thought I'd given you wrong directions on purpose . . ."

"Well, didn't you?" demanded Bob.

"No," said Ralph. "No, I didn't. You see, I'm not much good at reading. I can't read at all to myself, really, unless it's very, very easy – but I was ashamed to tell you I couldn't read those words in the old book and I just said what I thought, and it was wrong, of course."

There was silence for a minute. "I see," said Bob at last. "So you didn't even read that book after tea yesterday — the one you seemed to finish so quickly. You do tell dreadful stories, Ralph."

"I know. The thing is . . . I'm so big that people expect me to know a lot and I don't," said Ralph. "So I pretend, you see. And I was sorry tonight and I came to your room to tell you — but you were gone!"

"So you followed us," said Mary. "Well, I'm very glad you did, Ralph, or we'd have been here all night. I'm sorry we called you mean. We really and truly thought you read out wrong directions on purpose to stop us finding the door."

"I'm sorry too," said Bob, and solemnly held out his hand. The boys shook hands.

"I missed the adventure," said Ralph, sorrowfully.

"Never mind — you came in at the end of it," said Mary. "Now let's go and wake Granny!"

13

The End of the Adventure

The three children left the tiny hidy-hole behind them, and went in single file down the secret passage. They came at last to the little secret door that led into the study, behind the bookcase.

The moon still shone through the windows and Mary's jewellery sparkled even more brilliantly.

They went quietly up the stairs to Granny's bedroom and knocked on the door.

"Who's there?" said Granny's voice, sleepily.

"It's us – the twins and Ralph," said Bob.

"What's the matter? Is one of you ill?" called Granny. "Come in – the door isn't locked."

They heard a click as Granny put on her light. They opened the door and went in, still in their slippers and dressing-gowns.

Granny looked at them anxiously, thinking that one of them at least must be ill. She suddenly saw all the glittering jewellery that Mary had on.

"Mary! Where did you get all that?" she began. Then she saw the necklace. "Mary – that necklace! Good gracious, am I dreaming, or is that the lost necklace? I must be dreaming!"

"You're not, Granny," said Mary, coming close to the bed. "It is the lost necklace – look, it's the same one that is painted in all those portraits – with the big shiny pearls and everything!"

"My dear child!" said Granny, in wonder, and put out her hand to touch the gleaming pearls. "But where did you find these rings and brooches? Sit on my bed and tell me. I can't wait to hear!"

So the three of them cuddled into Granny's soft eiderdown and told their strange story – all about the plans in the old book, the mention of the

passage and the directions for finding the secret door and the hidy-hole where, most unexpectedly, they had found the jewellery in the little cubby-hole in the wall.

"I just can't believe it!" Granny kept saying. "I just can't. To think it was there, in a place that every single person had forgotten through all these years! And all these other treasures too. How I wish I knew the story of why they were hidden there – some thief, I suppose, stole them and put them in the safest place he knew and then couldn't get to them again!"

"Will they be yours, all these things, Granny?" asked Mary.

"The necklace certainly will, because it belongs to the family," said Granny, "and I expect the other things will too. Look, this ruby ring is the one painted on the finger of the third woman in the gallery of pictures!"

So it was. Mary remembered it quite well. She took off all the sparkling jewellery carefully and handed it to Granny. "That was a real adventure, wasn't it, Granny?" she said.

"It certainly was. Did you enjoy it too, Ralph?" asked Granny.

"Yes," said Ralph, hoping that the twins wouldn't tell that he had only come in at the last.

They didn't say a word. They were very sorry that Ralph hadn't shared all the adventure now. They felt much more kindly towards him, now they knew why he boasted and told such silly stories.

"You must go back to bed," said Granny, at last. "We'll talk about it all again tomorrow. It's too exciting for words!"

Everyone in the house was thrilled to hear about the midnight adventure. Cookie, who saw the bookcase out of its place early next morning, just couldn't believe it all.

"Well, well – it isn't often we have an adventure like this happening in Tall Chimneys!" she said. "I'll have to make a special cake to celebrate it!" So she did – and she actually made a beautiful necklace all round the cake, in white icing.

"Well, you will find the rest of your stay here rather dull, I'm afraid, after all this excitement," said Granny, when they sat down to their lunch in the middle of the day.

"No, we shan't," said Mary. "We're going to have a jolly good time with Ralph, aren't we, Bob? We're going to teach him to swim, and to row – and lots of other things!"

Ralph beamed. "Yes. I shan't need to show off and pretend then. Don't you worry, Granny – we're going to have a grand time here and I expect I'll be a lot nicer than I've been before."

"That's good news," said Granny. "You haven't always been nice, but I shall expect great things of you now."

They did have a grand time together, and Ralph learned a whole lot of things he didn't know before. The twins began to like him very much indeed.

Before they left Tall Chimneys, they all had a surprise. Granny said she wanted to give them goodbye presents.

"This is for you, Mary," she said, and gave the little girl a small sparkling brooch that had been in the lost jewellery. "I've had it cleaned and altered — and now it is just right for a little girl like you to wear at a party."

She turned to the boys. "And I've sold a little of the jewellery I didn't want to keep," she said, "and I have bought these watches, one for each of you — just to remind you of the adventure."

She gave them two splendid watches, and they put them on proudly. What would the boys at school say when they saw those?

"Thank you, Granny!" said the children, and hugged her. "We've had a simply lovely time — and we never, never will forget our adventure of the lost necklace."

MISCHIEF AT
ST ROLLO'S

1

A New School

"I don't want to go to boarding-school," said Michael.

"Neither do I," said Janet. "I don't see why we have to, Mum!"

"You are very lucky to be able to go," said Mother. "Especially together! We have chosen a mixed school for you, one with boys and girls together, so that both you and Mike can go together. We know how fond you are of one another. It's quite time you went too. I run after you too much. You must learn to stand on your own feet."

Mother went out of the room. The two children stared at one another. "Well, that's that," said Janet, flipping a pellet of paper at Michael. "We've got to go. But I vote we make our new school sit up a bit!"

"I've heard that you have to work rather hard at St Rollo's," said Mike. "Well I'm not going to! I'm going to have a good time. I hope we're in the same class."

There was only a year between the two of them, and as Janet was a clever child, she had so far always been in the same form as her brother, who was a year older. They had been to a mixed school ever since they had first started, and although they now had to go away to boarding-school, they both felt glad that they were not to be parted, as most brothers and sisters had to be.

The last week of the holidays flew past. Mother took the children to the shops to get them fitted for new clothes.

"We do seem to have to get a lot for our new school," said Janet, with interest. "And are we going to have tuck-boxes, Mum, to take back with us?"

"If you're good!" said Mother, with a laugh.

Mother did get them their tuck-boxes – one for each of them. She put exactly the same in each box – one big currant cake, one big ginger cake, twelve chocolate buns, a tin of toffee and a large bar of chocolate. The children were delighted.

The day came for them to go to their new school. They couldn't help feeling a bit excited, though they felt rather nervous too. Still, they were to go together, and that would be fun. They caught a train to London, and Mother took them to the station from which the school train was to start.

ST ROLLO'S SCHOOL, said the big blue label on the train. RESERVED FOR ST ROLLO'S SCHOOL. A great crowd of boys and girls were on the platform, talking and laughing, calling to each other. Some were new, and they looked rather lonely and shy. Janet and Mike kept together, looking eagerly at everyone.

"They look rather nice," said Mike to Janet. "I wonder which ones will be in our form."

Both boys and girls were in grey, and looked neat and smart. One or two masters and mistresses bustled up and down, talking to parents, and warning the children to take their places. Janet and Mike got into a carriage with several other boys and girls.

"Hello!" said one, a cheeky-looking boy of about eleven. "You're new, aren't you?"

"Yes," said Mike.

"What's your name?" said the boy, his blue eyes twinkling at Mike and Janet.

"I'm Michael Fairley, and this is my sister Janet," said Mike. "What's your name?"

"I'm Tom Young," said the boy. "I should think you'll be in my form. We have fun. Can you make darts?"

"Paper darts," said Mike. "Of course! Everybody can!"

"Ah, but you should see my new kind," said the

boy, and he took out a notebook with stiff paper leaves. But just as he was tearing out a sheet the guard blew his whistle and the train gave a jerk.

"Goodbye, Mum!" yelled Mike and Janet. "Goodbye. We'll write tomorrow!"

"Goodbye, my dears!" called Mother. "Enjoy yourselves and work hard."

The train left the station. Now that it was really gone the two children felt a bit lonely. It wasn't going to be very nice not to see their parents for some time. Thank goodness they had each other!

Tom looked at them. "Cheer up!" he said. "I felt like that, too, the first time. But you soon get over it. Now just see how I make my new paper darts."

Tom was certainly very clever with his fingers. In a minute or two he had produced a marvellous pointed dart out of paper, which, when it was thrown, flew straight to its mark.

"Better than most darts, don't you think?" said Tom proudly. "I thought that one out last term. The first time I threw one it shot straight at Miss Thomas and landed underneath her collar. I got sent out of the room for that."

Janet and Mike looked at Tom with much respect. All the other children in the carriage laughed.

"Tom's the worst boy in the school," said a big,

rosy-cheeked girl. "Don't take lessons from him – he just doesn't care about anything."

"Is Miss Thomas a mistress?" asked Mike. "Do we have masters and mistresses at St Rollo's?"

"Of course," said Tom. "If you're in my form you'll have Miss Thomas for class teacher, but a whole lot of other teachers for special subjects. I can tell you whose classes it's safe to play about in, and whose classes it's best to behave in."

"Well, seeing that you don't behave well in anybody's classes, I shouldn't have thought you could have told anyone the difference," said the big girl.

"Be quiet, Marian," said Tom. "I'm doing the talking in this carriage!"

That was too much for the other children. They fell on Tom and began to pummel him. But he took it all good-humouredly and pummelled back hard. Mike and Janet watched, laughing. They didn't quite like to join in.

Everyone had sandwiches to eat. They could eat them any time after half past twelve, but not before. Tom produced a watch after a while and looked at it.

"Good!" he said. "It's half past twelve." He undid his packet of sandwiches. Marian looked astonished.

"Tom! It simply can't be half past twelve yet," she said. She looked at her wristwatch. "It's only a quarter to."

"Well, your watch must be wrong then," said Tom, and he began to eat his sandwiches. Janet looked at her watch. It certainly was only a quarter to twelve. She felt sure that Tom had put his watch wrong on purpose.

It made the other children feel very hungry to watch Tom eating his ham sandwiches. They began to think it would be a good idea to put their watches fast, too! But just then a master came down the corridor that ran the length of the train. Tom tried to put away his packet of sandwiches, but he was too late.

"Well, Tom," said the master, stopping at the door and looking in. "Can't you wait to get to school before you begin to break the rules?"

"Mr Wills, sir, my watch says twenty-five to one," said Tom, holding out his watch, with an innocent look on his face. "Isn't it twenty-five to one?"

"You know quite well it isn't," said Mr Wills. He took the watch and twisted the hands back. "Put away your lunch and have it when your watch says half past twelve," he said. Tom gave a look at his watch. Then he looked up with an expression of horror. "Sir! You've made my watch half an hour slow! That would mean I couldn't start my lunch till one o'clock!"

"Well, well, fancy that!" said Mr Wills. "I wonder which is the more annoying – to have a watch that is fast, or one that is slow, Tom? What a pity! You'll have to eat your lunch half an hour after the others have finished!"

He went out. Tom stared after him gloomily. "I suppose he thinks that's funny," he said.

Tom put away his lunch, for he knew quite well that Mr Wills might be along again at any moment. At half past twelve all the other children took down their lunch packets and undid them eagerly, for they were hungry. Poor Tom had to sit and watch them eat. His watch only said twelve o'clock!

At one, when all the others had finished, he opened his lunch packet again. "Now, of course," he said, "I'm so terribly hungry that ham sandwiches, egg sandwiches, buttered scones with jam, ginger cake, an apple and some chocolate won't nearly do for me!"

The train sped on. It was due to arrive at half past two. When the time came near, Janet and Mike looked out of the windows eagerly. "Can we see St Rollo's from the train?" asked Janet.

"Yes. It's built on a hill," said Marian. "You'll see it out of that window. It's grey stone and it has towers at each end. In the middle of the building is a big archway. Watch out for it now, you'll soon see it."

The children looked out and, as Marian had said, they caught sight of their new school. It looked grand!

There it stood on the hill with big towers at each end, built of grey stone. Creeper climbed over most of the walls, and here and there a touch of red showed that when autumn came the walls would glow red with the crimson leaves.

The train slowed down at a little station. Everyone got out. Some big coaches were waiting in the little station yard. Laughing and shouting, the children piled into them. Their luggage was to follow in a van. The masters and mistresses climbed in last of all, and the coaches set off to St Rollo's.

They rumbled up the hill and came to a stop before the big archway. The school looked enormous, now that the children were so close to it. All the boys and girls clambered down from the coaches and went in at a big door.

The two children followed Tom up the stairs to a large and cheerful room, into which the

afternoon sun poured. A plump, smooth-cheeked woman was sitting there.

"Hello, Matron," said Tom, going in. "I've brought two new ones to see you. Are they in my dormitory? I hope they are."

"Well, I'm sorry for them if they are!" said Matron, getting out a big exercise book and turning the pages. "What are their names?"

"Michael and Janet Fairley," said Mike.

Matron found their names and ticked them off.

"Yes, Michael is in your dormitory, Tom," she said. "Janet is across the passage with Marian and the girls. I hope they will help you to behave better, not worse. And just remember what I told you last term – if you play any tricks on me this term I'll send you to the headmaster!"

Tom grinned. He took Mike's arm and led him away with Janet. "You'll soon begin to think I'm a bad lot!" he said. "Come on – I'll show you everything."

2

Settling Down

There was plenty to see at St Rollo's. The dormitories were lovely big rooms. Each child had a separate cubicle with white curtains to pull round their bed, their dressing-table, and small cupboard. The children's luggage was already in the dormitory when they got there.

"We'll unpack later," said Tom. "Look, that will be my bed. And yours can be next to mine, Mike, if I can arrange it. Look – let's pull your trunk into this cubicle, then no one else will take it."

They pulled the trunk across. Then Tom showed Janet her dormitory, across the passage. It was exactly the same as the boys, except that the beds had pink bedspreads instead of blue. After that, Tom showed them the classrooms, which were fine rooms, all with great windows looking out on the sunny playgrounds.

"This is our classroom, if you're in my form," said Tom. Janet and Mike liked the look of it very much.

"I had that desk there at the front, last term,"

said Tom, pointing to one. "I always try to choose one right at the back – but sooner or later I'm always made to sit at the front. People seem to think they have to keep an eye on me. Awfully tiresome!"

"I wonder where our desks will be," said Mike.

"Bag two, if you like," said Tom. "Just dump a few books in. Where do you want to sit?"

"I like being near the window, where I can look out," said Mike. "But I'd like to be where I can see you too, Tom!"

"Well, I shall try to bag a desk at the back as usual," said Tom. He took a few books from a bookshelf and dumped them into a desk in the back row by the window. "That can be your desk. That can be Janet's. And this can be mine! All in a row together."

Tom showed them the playgrounds and the hockey fields. He showed them the marvellous gym and the assembly hall where the school met every morning for prayers. He showed them the changing-rooms, where they changed for games, and the common-rooms where each class met out of school to read, write or play games. Janet and Mike began to feel they would lose their way if they had to find any place by themselves!

"We'll go and unpack now," said Tom. "And

then it'll be teatime. Good! We can all have things out of our tuck-boxes today."

They went to their dormitories to unpack. Janet parted from the two boys and went into hers. Marian was there, and she smiled at Janet.

"Hello," she said. "I saw Tom taking you round. He's a kind soul, but he'll lead you into trouble, if he can! Come and unpack. I'll show you where to put your things. I'm head of this dormitory."

Janet unpacked and stowed away her things into the drawers of the dressing-table, and hung her clothes in the cupboard. All the other girls were doing the same. Marian called to Janet.

"I say! Do you know any of the others here? That's Angie near to you. And this is Emily. And that shrimp is Katie. And here's Delia, who just simply can't help being top of the form, whether she tries or not!"

Delia laughed. She was a clever-looking girl, with large glasses on her nose. "We're all in the same form," she told Janet. "Is your brother in Tom Young's dormitory?"

"Yes," said Janet. "Will he be in my form too?"

"Yes, he will," said Delia. "All the four dormitories on this floor belong to the same form. Miss Thomas is our form mistress. She's nice but pretty strict. Only one person ever gets the better of her and that's Tom Young! He just simply doesn't care what he does – and he's always bottom. But he's nice."

Meanwhile Mike was also getting to know the boys in his dormitory. Tom was telling him about them.

"See that fellow with the cross-eyes and hooked nose? Well, that's John."

Mike looked round for somebody with cross-eyes and a hooked nose, but the boy that Tom pointed to had the straightest brown eyes and nose that Mike had ever seen! The boy grinned.

"I'm John," he said. "Don't take any notice of Tom. He thinks he's terribly funny."

Tom took no notice. "See that chap over there in the corner? The one with spots all over his face? That's Peter. He gets spots because he eats too many sweets."

"Shut up!" said Peter. He had one small spot on his chin. He was a big, healthy-looking boy, with bright eyes and red cheeks.

"And this great giant of a chap is George," said Tom, pointing to an undergrown boy with small shoulders. The boy grinned.

"You must have your joke, mustn't you?" he said amiably. "And now Mike whatever-your-name-is, let me introduce you to the world's greatest clown, the world's greatest idiot, Master Thomas Henry William Young, biggest duffer and dunce, and, by a great effort, the bottom of the form!"

Mike roared with laughter. Tom took it all in good part. He gave George a punch which the boy dodged cleverly.

There was one other boy in the room, but Tom said nothing about him. He was not a pleasant-looking boy. Mike wondered why Tom didn't tell him his name. So he asked for it.

"Who's he?" he said, nodding his head towards the boy, who was unpacking his things with rather a sullen face.

"That's Hugh," said Tom, but he said no more.

Hugh looked up. "Go on, say what you like," he said. "The new boy will soon know all about me, anyway! Be funny at my expense if you want to!"

"I don't want to," said Tom.

"Well, I'll tell him then," said the boy. "I'm a cheat! I cheated in the exams last term, and everyone knows it because Tom found it out and gave me away!"

"I didn't give you away," said Tom. "I've told you that before. I saw that you were cheating, and said nothing. But Miss Thomas found it out herself. Anyway, let's drop the subject of cheating this term. Cheat all you like. I don't care!"

Tom turned his back on Hugh. Mike felt very awkward. He wished he hadn't asked for the boy's name. John began to talk about the summer holidays and all he had done. Soon the others joined in, and when Hugh slipped out of the room no one saw him go.

"It should be about teatime now," said Tom, pulling out his watch. "Golly, no it isn't! Half an hour to go still! My word, what a swizz!"

Just then the tea-bell rang loudly, and Tom looked astonished. Mike laughed. "Don't you remember?" he said. "Mr Wills put your watch back half an hour?"

"So he did!" said Tom, looking relieved. He altered his watch again. "Well, come on," he said. "I could eat a mountain if only it was made of cake! Bring your tuck-box. What have you got in it? I'll share mine with you if you'll share yours with me. I've got a simply gorgeous chocolate cake."

It was fun, that first meal. All the children had brought goodies back in their tuck-boxes. They shared with one another, and the most enormous teas were eaten that day! Janet went to sit with Mike, and the two of them gave away part of all their cakes. In exchange they got slices of all kind of other cakes. By the time they got up from the tea table they couldn't eat another crumb!

"I hope we don't have to have supper!" said Mike. "I feel as if I don't want to eat again for a fortnight. But wasn't it scrumptious?"

The children had to go and see the headmaster and headmistress after tea. Both were grey-haired, and had kindly but rather stern faces. Mike and Janet felt very nervous and could hardly answer the questions they were asked.

"You will both be in the same form at first," said the headmaster, Mr Quentin. "Janet is a year younger, but I hear that she is advanced for her age. You will be in the second form."

"Yes, sir," said the children.

"We work hard at St Rollo's," said Miss Lesley, the headmistress. "But we play hard too. So you should have a good time and enjoy every day of the term. Remember our motto always, won't you: 'Not the least that we dare, but the most that we can.'"

"Yes, we will," said the two children.

"St Rollo's does all it can for its children," said Miss Lesley, "so it's up to you to do all you can for your school, too. You may go."

The children went. "I like the heads, don't you, Mike?" said Janet. "But I'm a bit afraid of them too. I shouldn't like to be sent to them for punishment."

"I bet Tom has!" said Mike. "Now, we've got to go and see Miss Thomas. Come on."

Miss Thomas was in their classroom, making out lists. She looked up as the two children came in.

"Well, Michael; well, Janet!" she said, with a smile. "Finding your way round a bit? It's difficult at first, isn't it? I've got your last reports here, and they are quite good. I hope you will do as well for me as you seem to have done for your last form mistress!"

"We'll try," said the children, liking Miss Thomas's broad smile and brown eyes.

"I'm bad at maths," said Janet.

"And my handwriting is pretty awful," said Michael.

"Well, we'll see what we can do about it," said Miss Thomas. "Now you can go back to the common-room with the others. You'll know it by the perfectly terrible noise that comes out of the door!"

The children laughed and went out of the room. "I think I'm going to like St Rollo's very much," said Janet happily. "Everybody is so nice. The girls in my dorm are fine, Mike. Do you like the boys in yours?"

"Yes, all except a boy called Hugh," said Mike, and he told Janet about the sulky boy. "I say — is this our common-room, do you think?"

They had come to an open door, out of which came a medley of noises. A record player was going, and someone was singing loudly to it, rather out of tune. Two or three others were shouting about something and another boy was hammering on the floor, though why, Janet and Mike couldn't imagine. They put their heads in at the door.

"This can't be our common-room," said Mike. "The children all look too big."

"Get out of here, tiddlers!" yelled the boy who

was hammering on the floor. "You don't belong here! Find the kindergarten!"

"What cheek!" said Janet indignantly, as they withdrew their heads and walked off down the passage. "Tiddlers, indeed!"

Round the next passage was a noise that was positively deafening. It came from a big room on the left. A radio was going full-tilt, and a record player, too, so that neither of them could be heard properly. Four or five children seemed to be having a fight on the floor, and a few others were yelling to them, telling them to "Go it!" and "Stick it!"

A cushion flew through the air and hit Janet on the shoulder. She threw it back. A girl raised her voice dolefully.

"Oh, do shut up! I want to hear the radio!"

Nobody took any notice. The girl shouted even more loudly; "I say, *I want to hear the radio*."

Somebody snapped off the record player, and the radio seemed to boom out even more loudly. There was dance music on it.

"Let's dance!" cried Peter, holding a cushion as if it were a partner. "Hello, Mike, hello Janet. Where on earth have you been? Come into our quiet, peaceful room, won't you? Don't stand at the door looking like two scared mice."

So into their common-room went the two

children, at first quite scared of all the noise around them. But gradually they got used to it, and picked out the voices of the boys and girls they knew, talking, shouting, and laughing together. It was fun. It felt good to be there all together like a big, happy family. The noise was nice too.

For an hour the noise went on, and then died down as the children became tired. Books were got out, and puzzles. The radio was turned down a little. The supper-bell went, and the children trooped down into the dining-hall. The first day was nearly over. A quiet hour after supper, and then bed. Yes − it was going to be nice at St Rollo's!

3

A Happy Time

Michael and Janet found things rather strange at first, but after two or three days St Rollo's began to seem quite familiar to them. They knew their way about by then — though poor Janet got quite lost the second day, looking for her classroom!

She opened the door of what she thought was her form-room only to find a class of big boys and girls taking painting. They sat round the room with their drawing-boards in front of them, earnestly drawing or painting a vase of bright leaves.

"Hello! What do you want?" asked the drawing-master.

"I wanted the second-form classroom," said Janet, blushing red.

"Oh well, this isn't it," said the master. "Go down the stairs, turn to the right and it's the first door."

"Thank you," said Janet, thinking how silly she was not to remember what floor her classroom was on. Flustered, she ran down the stairs, and tried to remember if the drawing-master had said turn to the left or to the right.

"I think he said left," said Janet to herself. So to the left she turned and opened the first door there. To her horror, it was the door of the junior mistresses' common-room! One or two of them sat there, making out timetables.

"What is it?" said the nearest one.

"Nothing," said Janet, going red again. "I'm looking for my classroom — the second form. I keep going into the wrong room."

"Oh, you're a new girl, aren't you?" said the mistress, with a laugh. "Well, go along the passage and take the first door on the right."

So at last Janet found her classroom, and was very relieved. But when three or four days had gone by she couldn't imagine how she could have made such a mistake! The school building, big as it was, was beginning to be very familiar to her.

The second form settled down well. Janet and Mike were the only new children in it. Miss Thomas let them keep the desks they had chosen — but she looked with a doubtful eye on Tom, when he sat down at the desk in the back row next to Janet.

"Oh," she said, "so you've chosen a desk in the back row again, Tom. Do you think it's worthwhile doing that? You know quite well that before a week has gone by you will be told to take a desk out here in front, where I can keep my eye on you."

"Oh, Miss Thomas!" said Tom. "I'm turning over a new leaf this term. Really I am. Let me keep this desk. I'm trying to help the new children, so I'm sitting by them."

"I see," said Miss Thomas, who looked as if she didn't believe a word that Tom said. "Well – I give you not more than a week there, Tom! We'll just see!"

There were a good many children in the second form. Mike and Janet soon got to know them all. They were a jolly lot, cheerful and full of fun – except for the boy called Hugh, who hardly spoke to anyone and seemed very sullen.

Tom was a great favourite. He made the silliest jokes, played countless tricks, and yet was always ready to help anyone. The teachers liked him, though they were forever scolding him for his careless work.

"It isn't necessary for you to be bottom of every subject, every week, is it, Tom?" said Miss Thomas. "I mean – wouldn't you like to give me a nice surprise and be top in something just for once?"

"Oh, Miss Thomas, would it really be a nice surprise?" said Tom. "Wouldn't it be a shock? I wouldn't like to give you a shock."

"Considering that you spend half your time thinking out tricks to shock people, that's a foolish remark!" said Miss Thomas. "Now, open your books at page nineteen."

Janet and Mike found the work to be about the same as they had been used to. They both had brains, and it was not difficult for them to keep up with the others. In fact, Janet felt sure that, if she tried very hard, she could be top of the form! She had a good memory, and usually didn't forget anything she had read or heard. This was a great gift, for it made all lessons easy for her.

Delia, the girl with glasses, was easily top each week. Nothing seemed difficult to her. Even the hot-tempered French master beamed on Delia and praised her – though he seldom praised anyone else. Mike and Janet were quite scared of him.

"Monsieur Crozier looked as if he was going to shout at me this morning!" said Janet to Mike. "Don't you think he did?"

"He will shout at you if you give him the slightest chance!" said Tom, with a grin. "He shouted at me so loudly last term that I almost jumped out of my skin. I just got back into it in time."

"Idiot!" said Mike. "I bet you'd played some sort of trick on him."

"He had," said Peter. "He put white paint on that front lock of his hair – and when Monsieur Crozier exclaimed about it, what do you suppose Tom said?"

"What?" said Janet and Mike together.

"He said, 'Monsieur Crozier, my hair is turning white with the effort of learning the French verbs you have given us this week,'" said Peter. "And do you wonder he got shouted at after that?"

"I'll think out something to make old Monsieur sit up!" said Tom. "You wait and see!"

"Oh, hurry up, then," begged the children around him.

A week or two passed by, and Mike and Janet settled down well. They loved everything. The work was not too difficult for them. The teachers were jolly. Hockey was marvellous. This was played three times a week, and everyone was expected to turn up. Gym was fine too. Mike and Janet were good at this, and enjoyed the half-hours in the big gym with the others.

There were lovely walks around the school. The children were allowed to go for walks by themselves, providing that three or more of them went together. So it was natural that Tom, Mike and Janet should often go together. The other children made up threes too, and went off for an hour or so when they could. It was lovely on the hills around, and already the children were looking for ripe blackberries and peering at the nut trees to see if there were going to be many nuts.

"Doesn't Hugh ever go for a walk?" said Janet once, when she, Mike and Tom had come in from a lovely sunny walk, to find Hugh bent double over a book in a far corner of the common-room. He was alone. All the other children were out doing something – either practising hockey on the field, or gardening, or walking.

"Well, there has to be at least three of you to go for a walk," said Tom in a low voice. "And no one ever asks Hugh, of course – and he wouldn't like to ask two others because he'd be pretty certain they'd say no."

"Why does everyone dislike him so?" asked Janet. "He would be quite a nice-looking boy if only he didn't look so surly."

"He was new last term," said Tom. "He's not very clever, but he's an awful swot – mugs up all sorts of things, and always has his nose in a book. Won't join in things, you know. And when he cheated at the exams last term, that was the last straw. Nobody decent wanted to have anything to do with him."

"He can't be very happy," said Janet, who was a

kind-hearted girl, willing to be friends with anyone.

"Perhaps he doesn't deserve to be," said Tom.

"But even if you don't deserve to be happy, it must be horrid never to be," argued Janet.

"Oh, don't start being a ministering angel, Janet," said Mike impatiently. "Don't you remember how sorry you were for that spiteful dog next door, who was always being told off for chasing hens? Well, what happened when you went out of your way to be kind to him, because you thought he must be miserable? He snapped at you, and nearly took your finger off!"

"I know," said Janet. "But that was only because he couldn't understand anyone being kind to him."

"Well, Hugh would certainly snap your head off if you tried any kind words on him," said Tom, with a laugh. "Look out – here he comes."

The children fell silent as Hugh got up from his seat and made his way to the door. He had to pass the three on his way, and he looked at them sneeringly.

"Talking about me, I suppose?" he said. "Funny how everyone stops talking when I come near!"

He bumped rudely into Janet as he passed and sent her against the wall. The two boys leaped at

Hugh, but he was gone before they could hold him.

"Well, do you feel like going after him and being sweet?" said Tom to Janet. She shook her head. She thought Hugh was horrid. But all the same she was sorry for him.

Mike and Janet wrote long letters to their mother and father.

We're awfully glad we came to St Rollo's, wrote Mike. *It's such fun to be with boys and girls together, and as Janet is in my form, we are as much together as ever we were. I shouldn't be surprised if she's top one week. The hockey is lovely. I'm good at it. Do send us some chocolate, if you can.*

His mother and father smiled at his letters and Janet's. They could see that the two children were happy at the school they had chosen for them and they were glad.

St Rollo's is fine, wrote Janet. *I am glad we came here. We do have fun!*

They certainly did – and they meant to have even more fun very soon!

4

Tom is Up to Tricks

Tom was always up to tricks. He knew all the usual ones, of course – the trick of covering a bit of paper with ink on one side, and handing it to someone as if it were a note, and then, when they took it they found their fingers all inky! He knew all the different ways of making paper darts. He knew how to flip a pellet of paper, from underneath his desk so that it would land exactly where he wanted it. There was nothing that Tom didn't know, when it came to tricks!

He lasted just four days in his desk at the back. Then Miss Thomas put him well in the front!

"I thought you wouldn't last a week at the back there," she said. "I feel much more comfortable with you just under my eye! Ah – that's better. Now I think you will find it quite difficult to fire off your paper pellets at children who are really trying to work."

The trick that had made Miss Thomas move him had caused the class a good deal of merriment. Miss Thomas had written history questions on the board for the form to answer in writing. Janet was hard at work answering them, for she wanted to get good marks, and Mike was working well too.

Suddenly Janet felt a nudge. She looked up. Tom had already finished answering the questions, though Janet felt certain that he had put "I don't know" to some of them! Tom nodded his head towards the window.

Janet looked there. Just outside was one of the gardeners, hard at work in a bed. He was a large man, red-faced, with a very big nose.

"What about giving old Nosey a shock?" said Tom, opening his desk to speak behind it. Janet nodded gleefully. She didn't know what Tom meant to do, but she was sure it would be funny.

Tom hunted in his desk till he found what he wanted. It was a piece of clay. The boy shut his desk and warmed the clay in his hands below it. It soon became soft and he picked off pieces to make hard pellets.

Janet and Mike watched him. Miss Thomas looked up. "Janet! Michael! Tom! Have you all finished your questions? Then get out your text-books and learn the list on page twenty-three."

The children got out their books. Tom winked at Janet. He waited until Miss Thomas was standing at Peter's desk, with her back turned to him, and then, very deftly, he flicked the clay pellet out of the open window with his thumb.

It hit the gardener on the top of his hat. He thought something had fallen on him from above and he stood up, raising his head to the sky, as if he thought it must be raining. Janet gave a muffled giggle.

"Shut up," whispered Tom. He waited till the man had bent down again, and his big nose presented a fine target. Flick! A big pellet flew straight out of the window and this time it hit the astonished man right on the tip of his nose, with a smart tap.

He stood up straight, rubbing his nose, glaring into the window. But all he saw were bent heads and innocent faces, though one little girl was certainly smiling very broadly to herself. That was Janet, of course. She simply could not keep her mouth from smiling!

The gardener muttered something to himself, glared at the bent heads, and bent over his work again. Tom waited for his chance and neatly flicked out another pellet. It hit the man smartly on the cheek, and he gave a cry of pain.

All the children looked up. Miss Thomas gazed in surprise at the open window, outside which the gardener was standing.

"Now, look here!" said the angry man, staring in at the window. "Which of you did that? Hitting me in the face with peas or something! Where's your teacher?"

"I'm here," said Miss Thomas. "What is the matter? I don't think any of the children here have been playing tricks. You must have made a mistake. Please don't disturb the class."

"Made a mistake! Do you suppose I don't know when anyone is flicking peas or something at me?" said the gardener. He glared at Janet, who was giggling. "Yes — and that's the girl who did it, too, if you ask me! She was giggling to herself before and I'm pretty certain I saw her doing it."

"That will do," said Miss Thomas. "I will deal with the matter myself. I am sorry you have been hindered in your work."

She shut down the window. The man went off, grumbling. Miss Thomas looked at Janet, who was very red.

"Kindly leave the gardeners to do their work, Janet," she said in a cold voice. "Bring your things out of your desk and put them in the empty front one. You had better sit there, I think."

Janet didn't know what to say. She couldn't give Tom away, and if she said she hadn't done it, Miss Thomas would ask who did, and then Tom would get into trouble. So with a lip that quivered, Janet opened her desk and began to get out her things.

Tom spoke up at once. "It wasn't Janet," he said. "I did it. I didn't like the look of the gardener's nose so I just hit it with a clay pellet or two, Miss Thomas. I'm sure you would have liked to do it yourself, Miss Thomas, if you had seen that big nose out there."

Everyone choked with laughter. Miss Thomas didn't even smile. She looked straight at Tom with cold eyes.

"I hope my manners are better than yours," she said. "If not, I don't know what I should feel inclined to do to you, Tom Young. Bring your things out here, please. You will be under my eye in future."

So, with many soft groans, Tom left his seat at the back beside Janet, and went to the front.

"Oh, what a pity," said Janet, later on, as the class was waiting for Monsieur Crozier to come. "Now you won't be able to do any more tricks, Tom. You're right at the front."

"Goodness, you don't think that will stop Tom, do you?" said Peter. And Peter was right. It didn't!

Monsieur Crozier was not a very good person to play about with, because he had such a hot temper. The class never knew how he was going to take a joke. Sometimes, if Tom or Marian said something sharp, he would throw back his grey head and roar with laughter. Yet at other times he could not see a joke at all, but would fly into a temper.

Few people dared to play tricks on the French master, but Tom, of course, didn't care what he did. One morning, Janet and Mike found him kneeling down in a far corner of the room, behind the teacher's desk. In this corner stood two or three rolled-up maps. Tom was hiding something behind the maps.

"Whatever are you doing?" asked Janet in surprise. Tom grinned.

"Preparing a little surprise packet for dear Monsieur Crozier," he said.

"What is it?" said Mike, peering down.

"Quite simple," said Tom. "Look – I've got two empty cotton-reels here and I've tied thin black thread to each. If you follow the thread you'll see it runs behind this cupboard, behind that bookcase, over the hot-water pipe, and up to my desk. Now, what will happen when I pull the threads?"

"The cotton-reels will dance in their corner!" giggled Janet, "and Monsieur Crozier won't know what the noise is – because over here is far from where anyone sits! What fun!"

Mike told everyone what was going to happen. It was a small trick but might be very funny. The whole class was excited. In the French lesson that day they were to recite their French verbs, which was a very dull thing to do. Now it looked as if the lesson wouldn't be dull after all.

Monsieur Crozier came into the room, his spectacles on his nose. His hair was untidy. It was plain that he had been in a temper with somebody, for it was his habit to ruffle his hair whenever he was angry. It stood up well, and the class smiled to see it.

"*Asseyez-vous!*" rapped out Monsieur Crozier, and the class sat down at once. In clear French sentences the master told them what he expected of them. Each child was to stand in turn and recite the French verb he had been told to learn, and the others were to write them out.

"And this morning I expect hard work!" said the French master. "I have had disgraceful work from the third form – disgrrrrrrrraceful! I will not put up with the same thing from you. You understand?"

"Yes, Monsieur Crozier," chanted the class. Monsieur Crozier looked at Tom, who had on a most innocent expression that morning.

"And you, too, will work!" he said. "It is not

necessary always to be bottom. If you had no brains I would say, "Ah, the poor boy – he cannot work!" But you have brains and you will not use them. That is bad, very bad."

"Yes, sir," said Tom.

Monsieur Crozier gave a grunt and sat down. Peter stood up to recite his verbs. The rest of the class bent over their desks to write them. They were all listening for Tom to begin his trick. He did nothing at first, but waited until Peter had sat down. There was silence for a moment, while the French master marked Peter's name in his book.

Then Tom pulled at the threads which ran to his desk. At once the cotton-reels over in the far corner

began to jiggle like mad. *Jiggle, jiggle, jiggle,* they went. *Jiggle, jiggle, jiggle!*

Monsieur Crozier looked up, puzzled. He didn't quite know where the noise came from. He stared round the quiet class. Everyone's head was bent low, for most of the children were trying to hide their smiles. Janet felt a giggle coming and she shut her mouth hard. She was a terrible giggler. Mike looked at her anxiously. Janet so often gave the game away by exploding into a tremendous laugh.

The noise stopped. Delia stood up to say her verbs. She was quite perfect in them. She sat down. Monsieur Crozier marked her name. Tom pulled at the threads and the cotton-reels jerked madly about behind the maps.

"What is that noise?" said the master impatiently, looking round. "Who makes that noise?"

"What noise, sir?" asked Tom innocently. "Is there a noise? I heard an aeroplane pass over just now."

"An aeroplane does not make a noise in this room!" said the master. "It is a jiggling noise. Who is doing it?"

"A jiggling noise, sir?" said Mike, looking surprised. "What sort of jiggling noise? My desk is a bit wobbly, sir – perhaps it's that you heard?"

Mike wobbled his desk and made a terrific noise. Everyone laughed.

"Enough!" cried Monsieur Crozier, rapidly losing his temper. "It is not your desk I mean. Silence! We will listen for the noise together."

There was a dead silence. Tom did not pull the threads. There was no noise at all.

But as soon as John was standing up, reciting his verbs in his soft voice, Tom jerked hard at his threads, and the reels did a kind of dance behind the maps, sounding quite loud on the boards.

"There is that noise again!" said the master angrily. "Silence, John. Listen!"

Tom could not resist making the reels dance again as everyone listened. *Jiggle-jiggle-jiggle-tap-tap-tap-jiggle-jiggle* they went, and the class began to giggle.

"It comes from behind those maps," said the French master, puzzled. "It is very strange."

"Mice, perhaps, sir," said Mike. Tom flashed him a grin. Mike was playing well.

The French master did not like mice. He stared at the maps, annoyed. He did not see how the noise could possibly be a trick, for the maps were far from any child's desk.

"Shall I see, sir?" asked Tom, getting up. "I don't mind mice a bit. I think Mike may be right, sir. It certainly does sound like a mouse caught behind there. Shall I look, sir?"

Now, what Tom thought he would do was to look behind the maps, pocket the reels quickly after pulling the threads away, and then announce that there was no mouse there. But when he got to the corner, he couldn't resist carrying the trick a bit further.

"I'll pretend there really is a mouse!" he thought. "That'll give the class a real bit of fun!"

So, when he knelt down and fiddled about behind the maps, pulling away the threads and getting hold of the cotton-reels, he suddenly gave a yell that made everyone jump, even the French master. "It's a mouse! It's a mouse! Come here, you bad little thing! Sir, it's a mouse!"

The class knew perfectly well it wasn't. Janet gave a loud, explosive giggle that she tried hastily to turn into a cough. Even the surly Hugh smiled.

Tom knocked over all the maps, pretending to get the mouse. Then he made it seem as if the little creature had run into the classroom, and he jumped and bounded after the imaginary mouse, crawling under desks and nearly pulling a small table on top of him. The whole class exploded into a gale of laughter that drowned Monsieur Crozier's angry voice.

"Come here, you!" yelled Tom, thoroughly enjoying himself. "Ah – got you! No, I haven't! Just touched your tail. Ah, there you are again. Whoops! Nearly got you that time. What a mouse! Oh, what a mouse! Whoops, there you go again!"

Mike got out of his desk to join him. The two boys capered about on hands and knees and nearly drove Monsieur Crozier mad. He hammered on his desk. But it was quite impossible for the class to be silent. They laughed till their sides ached.

And in the middle of it all Miss Thomas walked in, furious! She had been taking the class next door, and could not imagine what all the noise was. She had felt certain that no teacher was with the second form. She stopped in surprise when she saw Monsieur Crozier there, red in the face with fury.

The class stopped giggling when they saw Miss Thomas. She had a way of giving out rather unpleasant punishments, and the class somehow felt that she could not readily believe in their mouse.

"I'm sorry, Monsieur Crozier," said Miss Thomas. "I thought you couldn't be here."

"Miss Thomas, I dislike your class," said Monsieur Crozier, quite as ready to fly into a temper with Miss Thomas as with the children.

"They are ill-disciplined, ill-behaved, ill-mannered. See how they chase a mouse round your classroom! Ah, the bad children!"

"A mouse!" said Miss Thomas, in the utmost surprise. "But how could that be? There are no mice in the school. The school cats see to that. Has anyone got a tame mouse, then?"

"No, Miss Thomas," chorused the children together.

"We heard a noise behind the maps," began Tom, but Miss Thomas silenced him with a look.

"Oh, you did, did you?" she said. "You may as well know that I don't believe in your mouse, Tom. I will speak to you all at the beginning of the next lesson. Pardon me for coming in like this, Monsieur Crozier. I apologise also for my class."

The class felt a little subdued. The French master glared at them, and proceeded to give them so much homework that they would have groaned if they had dared. Tom got shouted at when he opened his mouth to protest. After that, he said no more. Monsieur Crozier was dangerous when he got as far as shouting!

Miss Thomas was very sarcastic about the whole affair when she next saw her class. She flatly refused to believe in the mouse, but instead asked who had gone to examine the noise in the corner.

"I did," said Tom, who always owned up to anything, quite fearlessly.

"I thought so," said Miss Thomas. "Well, you will write me an essay, four pages long, on the habits of mice, Tom. Give it to me this evening."

"But Miss Thomas," began Tom, "you know it's the hockey match this afternoon, and we're all watching it, and after tea there's a concert."

"That doesn't interest me at all," said Miss Thomas. "What interests me intensely at the moment is the habits of mice, and that being so, I insist on having that essay by seven o'clock. Not another word, Tom, unless you also want to write me an essay on, let us say, cotton-reels. I am not quite so innocent as Monsieur Crozier."

After that there was no more to be said. Mike and Janet gave up watching the hockey match in order to help Tom with his essay. Mike looked up the habits of mice, and Janet looked up the spelling of the words. With many groans and sighs Tom managed to write four pages in his largest handwriting by seven o'clock. "It is decent of you to help," he said gratefully.

"Well, we shared the fun, didn't we?" said Mike. "So we must share the punishment too!"

5

An Exciting Idea

In the middle of that term Mike's birthday came. He was very much looking forward to it because he knew he would have plenty of presents sent to him, and he hoped his mother would let him have a large birthday cake.

"I hope it won't be broken in pieces before it arrives," he said to Janet. "You know, Peter had a birthday last term, and he said his cake came in crumbs and they had to eat it with a spoon. I'd better warn Mum to pack it very carefully."

But Mother didn't risk packing one. She wrote to Mike and told him to order himself a cake from the big cake shop in the town nearby.

And if you would like to give a small party to your own special friends, do so, she said. *You can order what you like in the way of food and drink, and tell the shop to send me the bill. I can trust you not to be too extravagant, I know. Have a good time, and be sure your birthday cake has lots of icing on.*

Mike was delighted. He showed the letter to Tom. "Isn't Mum decent!" he said. "Can you come down to the town with Janet and me today, Tom, and help me to order things?"

"You're not going to ask all the boys and girls in the class to share your party, are you?" said Tom. "You know that would cost your mother a small fortune."

"Would it?" said Mike. "Well – what shall I do, then? How shall I choose people without making the ones left out feel hurt?"

"Well, if I were you, I'd just ask the boys in your own dormitory, and the girls in Janet's," said Tom. "That will be quite enough children."

"Yes, that's a good idea," said Mike, pleased. "I wish we could have our party in a separate room, so that the others we haven't asked won't have to see us eating the birthday cake and the other things. That would make me feel rather mean."

"Well, listen," said Tom, looking excited. "Why not have a midnight feast? We haven't had one for two terms. It's about time we did."

"A midnight feast!" said Janet, her eyes nearly popping out of her head. "Oooh, that would be marvellous. I've read about them in books. Oh Mike, do let's have your party in the middle of the night. Do, do!" Mike didn't need much pressing. He was just as keen on the idea as Janet and Tom! The three of them began to talk excitedly about what they would do.

"Shall we have it in one of our dormitories?" said Janet. "Either yours or mine, Mike?"

"No," said Tom at once. "Mr Wills sleeps in the room next to ours – and Miss Thomas sleeps in the room next to yours, Janet. Either of them might hear us making a noise and come and find us."

"We needn't make a noise," said Janet. "We could just eat and drink."

"Janet! You couldn't possibly last an hour or two without going off into one of your giggling fits, you know you couldn't," said Mike. "And you make an awful noise with your first giggle. It's like an explosion."

"I know," said Janet. "I can't help it. I smother it till I almost burst and then it comes out all of a sudden. Well – if we don't have the feast in one of our dormitories, where shall we have it?"

They all thought hard. Then Tom gave a grin. "I know the very place. What about the gardeners' shed?"

"The gardeners' shed!" said Mike and Janet together. "But why there?"

"Well, because it's out of the school and we can make a noise," said Tom. "And because it's not far from the little side door we use when we go to the playing-fields. We can easily slip down and open it to go out. And also, it would be a good place to store the food in. We can put it into boxes and cover them with sacks."

"Yes – it does sound rather good," said Mike. "It would be marvellous to be out of the school building, because I'm sure we'd make a noise."

"Last time we had a midnight feast, we had it in a dormitory," said Tom. "And in the middle someone dropped a ginger-beer bottle. We got so frightened at the noise that we all hopped into bed, and the feast was spoilt. If we hold ours in the shed, we shan't be afraid of anyone coming. Let's!"

So it was decided to hold it there. Then the next excitement was going down to the town to buy the food.

They went to the big cake shop first. Mike said what he wanted. "I want a big birthday cake made," he said. "Enough for about twelve people, please. And I want it to be covered with pink icing, and written on it in white I'd like 'A happy birthday'. Can you do that?"

"Certainly," said the shopgirl, and wrote down Mike's name, and his mother's address, so that she could send her the bill. Then Mike turned to the others. "What else shall we have?" he said. "You help me to choose."

So Janet and Tom obligingly helped him, and between them they chose chocolate cakes, biscuits, shortbread and currant buns. Then they went to the grocer's and asked for tinned sweetened milk, which everyone loved, sardines, tinned pineapple, and bottles of lemonade and ginger-beer.

The shop promised to pack up the goods and have them ready for the children to collect on the morning of Mike's birthday. The children meant to go down immediately after morning school and fetch the things.

They felt very excited. Janet and Mike counted up the cakes and things they had ordered and felt sure they had bought enough to feed everyone very well indeed.

"And now we'll have to ask everyone," said Mike happily. "Isn't it fun to invite people, Janet?"

"I'll ask the girls in my dorm tonight," said Janet. "The rest of the class won't be there then, so they won't know. I vote we don't tell anyone except our guests that we're going to have a feast. We don't want it to get to the ears of any of the teachers. Tell the boys in your dorm to keep it quiet, Mike."

"Right," said Mike. Then he frowned. "I say, Janet," he said, "what about Hugh? Are we to ask him?"

Janet stared at Mike. She didn't know what to say. "Well, I suppose we'd better," she said at last. "It would be rather awful to leave him out as he belongs to your dormitory. No one likes him but still he'd feel simply awful if he knew we were having a feast and he hadn't been asked."

"All right," said Mike. "I'll ask him. But he's such a surly fellow that he'll be an awful wet blanket."

Tom agreed that Hugh must be asked too. "I don't want him," he said, "but, after all, he belongs to our dorm, and it would make him feel pretty dreadful to be left out when everyone else is going."

So Mike quite meant to ask Hugh too. But then, something happened to make him change his mind. It had to do with Tom, and it happened in Mr Wills's class.

Mr Wills was taking maths with the second form. Tom was bored. He hated maths, and seldom got a sum right. Mr Wills had almost given up on him. So long as Tom sat quietly at his desk and didn't disturb the others, Mr Wills left him in peace. But if Tom got up to any tricks Mr Wills pounced on him.

Tom usually behaved himself in the maths class, for he respected Mr Wills, and knew that he would stand no nonsense. But that morning he was restless. He had slept very well the night before and was so full of beans that he could hardly sit still. He had prepared a trick for the French master in the next lesson, and was longing to play it.

The trick was one of his string tricks. He was marvellous at those. He had slipped into the classroom before school that morning and had neatly tied strong yellow thread to the pegs that held the blackboard on its easel. A jerk at the thread and a peg would come out – and down would crash the blackboard!

Tom looked at Mr Wills. Mr Wills caught his eye and frowned. "Get on, Tom," he said. "Don't slack so. If you can't get a sum right, get it wrong. Then, at least, I shall know you've been doing something!"

"Yes, Mr Wills," said Tom meekly. He scribbled down a few figures that meant nothing at all. His hand itched to pull away the peg. As his desk was at the front, he could easily leap forward and pick up the peg before Mr Wills could see that string was tied to it.

"It's a bit dangerous to try it on with Mr Wills," thought Tom. "But I'm so bored I must do something!"

He turned round and caught Mike's eye. Mike winked. Tom winked back, then he winked twice with each eye in turn. That was his signal to Mike that a trick was about to be played! Mike nudged Janet. They both looked up eagerly. Hugh caught their eager looks and wondered what was up. He guessed that Tom was about to play a trick and he watched him.

Mr Wills was at the back of the room, looking at Emily's work. Tom jerked his thread. The peg of the easel flew out, one side of the blackboard slipped down, and then it fell with a resounding crash on to the floor, making everyone jump violently. Mike and Janet knew what had happened, and they tried not to laugh. Hugh also saw what had happened. Before anyone could do anything Tom was out of his desk in a flash, and had picked up the blackboard and peg and set them back in place. He wondered whether or not to remove the threads, but decided he would risk it again.

"Thank you, Tom," said Mr Wills, who hadn't for a moment guessed that it was a trick. "Get on with your work, everybody."

Most of the children guessed that it was Tom up to his tricks again. They watched to see if it would happen once more. Mr Wills went to see Hugh's work. He had done most of his sums wrong, and the master grumbled at him.

"You haven't been trying! What have you been thinking of to put down this sum like that! No one else in the class has so many sums wrong!"

Hugh flushed. He always hated being grumbled at in front of anyone. "I'm sure Tom has more sums wrong than I have," he said, in a low voice.

At that moment Tom jerked both pegs neatly out of the easel and the board fell suddenly, with an even greater crash than before. Everyone giggled and Janet gave one of her explosions. The noise she made caused the children to laugh even more loudly.

"What's the matter with the board this morning?" said Mr Wills irritably.

"I should think Tom has something to do with it," said Hugh spitefully. "You'll find he hasn't got a single sum right and has given all his attention to our blackboard instead. I have at least been working!"

There was a silence. Mr Wills went to the blackboard. He examined the pegs. But they now had no thread on them, for Tom had slipped it off and it was safely in his pockets.

But not very safely, after all! Mr Wills turned to Tom. "Just turn out your pockets, please," he ordered. Tom obeyed promptly – and there on the desk lay the tell-tale yellow thread, still with the little slip-knots at one end.

"I'll see you after the class, Tom," said Mr Wills.

"I can't make you do good work but I can at least stop you from preventing the others from working. You should know by now that I don't stand any nonsense in my classes."

"Yes, sir," said Tom dolefully.

"Maths is a most important subject," went on Mr Wills. "Some of the children here are working for scholarships and it is necessary they should get on well this term. If you disturb my classes once more I shall refuse to have you in them."

"Yes, sir," said Tom again, going red. Mr Wills had a very rough tongue. When the master had turned his back on the class to write something on the now steady blackboard, Tom turned round to get the comfort of a look from Mike and Janet. They nodded at him – and then Tom caught sight of Hugh's face.

Hugh wore a spiteful grin on his face. He was pleased to have got Tom into trouble.

"Sneak!" whispered Mike to Hugh.

"Silence!" said Mr Wills, not turning round. Mike said no more, but gave Hugh a look that said all his tongue longed to say!

"Wait till after school!" said the look. "Just wait till after school."

6

Midnight Feast!

Tom got a tremendous scolding after the class, and entered the French class four minutes late, with a very red face. Monsieur Crozier looked at him in surprise. "And why are you late?" he said. "It is not the custom to walk into my classes after they have started."

"Please, sir, I'm sorry," said Tom, "but Mr Wills was talking to me."

The French master guessed that Tom had been up for a scolding, and he said no more. Tom was very subdued that lesson. Mr Wills had said some cutting things to him, and the boy felt rather ashamed of himself. It was all very well to play tricks and have a good time – but there was work to do as well! So he sat like a lamb in the French class, and really listened to the lesson.

After school, Mike, Janet and Peter went after Hugh. "Sneak!" said Mike furiously. "What did you want to go and give Tom away for?"

"Why shouldn't I?" said Hugh. "He sneaked on me last term."

"No, he didn't," said Mike. "He says he didn't – and you know as well as anybody that Tom's truthful. He doesn't tell lies. You're a beastly sneak!"

"Oh, shut up," said Hugh rudely, and walked off. But the others walked after him, telling him all kinds of truthful but horrid things about himself. Hugh went into a music room to practise and banged the door on them. He even turned the key in the lock.

"He really is a spiteful sneak," said Janet. "Mike, you're surely not going to ask him to our feast now, are you?"

"You bet I'm not," said Mike. "As if I'd have a sneaky creature like that on my birthday night! No fear!"

"Well, we'll ask all the others, and we'll warn them not to say a word to Hugh," said Janet. So they asked everyone else – Peter, John, small George, Marian, Emily, Katie, Angie and Delia. With Mike, Janet and Tom there would be eleven children altogether.

"And don't say a single word to anyone outside our dormitories," said Mike. "And don't say anything to Hugh, either. He's such a sneak that I'm not asking him. I'm sure if he got to know we were having a feast he'd prowl round and then tell about it! So, not a word, mind!"

Mike's birthday came. He had a lot of cards and many presents. A good deal of it was money and he meant to spend it in the holidays. His mother and father sent him a new paintbox and pencil-box with his name on them. His grandfather wrote to say that he had bought him a new bicycle. Janet gave him a box of writing paper and stamps. The others gave him small presents, pencils, rubbers, sweets, and so on. Mike was very happy.

"After school, we'll pop down with baskets and get all those things," he said. "We'd better ask one or two of the others to come too. We'll never be able to carry all the stuff ourselves."

So Peter and Marian came too, and the five set off with giggles and talk. They came back with all the food and drink, and undid the birthday cake in the gardeners' shed. It was simply marvellous.

A HAPPY BIRTHDAY was written across it, and the pink icing was thick and not too hard. It was a big cake. The children were delighted. Mike put it carefully back into its box.

The gardeners' shed was a big place. It was piled with boxes, tools, pots, wood and so on. Actually it was not much used, for the gardeners had another, smaller, shed they preferred, and they used the big shed mostly as a storehouse. The children soon found a good hiding-place for their food and drink. There was an enormous old packing-case, made of wood, at the back of the shed. They put everything into this and then put a board on top. On the board they piled rows of flowerpots.

"There," said Mike. "I don't think anyone would guess what is under those pots! Now, let's arrange what we're going to sit on."

There were plenty of boxes and big flowerpots. The children pulled them out and arranged them to sit on. "We shall have to pin sacks across the windows," said Mike. "Else the light of our candles and torches will be seen."

"Better do that this evening," said Tom. "It might make people suspicious if they came by and saw sacks across the windows."

So they left the windows uncurtained. There was nothing else they could do except smuggle in a few mugs and plates and spoons. Janet said she could do this with Marian. She knew where the school crockery was kept, and she could easily slip into the big cupboard after craftwork that afternoon and get what was needed. They could wash it after the feast and put it back again.

"I think that's everything," said Mike happily. "I say – this is going to be fun, isn't it! I can hardly wait till tonight!"

"I'll wake the girls in my dorm," said Janet, "and you wake the boys, Mike. Don't wake Hugh by mistake, though!"

Everything went off as planned. Janet fell asleep, but awoke just before midnight. She switched on her torch and looked at her watch. Five minutes to twelve! She slipped out of bed, put on socks, shoes, her underwear under her night-dress, and her jersey over it. Then her dressing-gown on top. She woke the other girls one by one, shaking them and whispering into their ears.

"It's time! Wake up! The midnight feast is about to begin!"

The girls awoke, and sat up, excited. They began to put on socks and jerseys too. Meanwhile the boys were doing the same thing. Mike had awoken them all, except, of course, Hugh, and in silence they were dressing. They did not dare to whisper, as the girls could, because they were afraid of waking Hugh.

They all crept out of the dormitory, and found the six girls waiting for them in the passage outside. Janet was trying to stop her giggles.

"For goodness sake don't do one of your explosions till we're out in the shed," said Mike anxiously. So Janet bit her lips together and waited. They all went down the stairs and out of the little side door. Then across to the big shed. Mike opened the door and everyone filed in. Once the door was shut, the children felt safe and began to talk in loud whispers.

Mike and Tom quickly put sacks across the three windows, and then lit three candles. Their wavering light made peculiar shadows in the shed, and everything looked rather mysterious and

exciting. The other children watched Mike and Tom go to the box at the back and lift off the flowerpots arranged there.

And then out came the good things to eat and drink! How the children gasped to see them! They all felt terribly hungry, and were pleased to see so much to eat and drink.

Mike set the birthday cake down on a big box. All the children crowded round to look at it. They thought it was marvellous. "We'll cut it as the very last thing," said Mike. "And don't forget to wish, everybody, because it's a birthday cake!"

They made a start on sardines and cake. It was a lovely mixture. Then they went on to currant buns, and biscuits, pineapple and tinned milk. They chattered in low voices and giggled to their hearts' content. When Peter fell off his box and upset sticky tinned milk all over himself, there was a gale of laughter. Peter looked so funny with his legs in the air, and milk dripping all over him!

"Sh! Sh!" said Mike. "Honestly, we'll wake up the whole school! Shut up, Janet! Your giggles make everyone worse still. You just make me want to giggle myself."

"This is the best feast we've ever had," said Tom, helping himself to a large piece of chocolate cake. "Any more ginger-pop, Mike?"

"Yes," said Mike. "Help yourself — and now, what about cutting the grand birthday cake?"

"It looks big enough for the whole school," Marian said giggling. "I say — I wish Hugh knew what he was missing! Wouldn't he be wild! I expect he is still sound asleep in his bed."

But Hugh wasn't! He had awakened at about half past twelve, and had turned over to go to sleep again. And then something strange had struck him. There was something missing in the dormitory. It was quite dark there and the boy could see nothing. But he lay there, half-asleep, wondering what was missing.

Then suddenly he knew. There was no steady breathing to be heard. There was no sound at all. Hugh sat up, alarmed. Why was nobody breathing? That was the usual sound to be heard at night, if anyone woke up. What had happened?

Hugh switched on his torch and got out of bed. He looked round the curtains that separated his cubicle from the next boy's. The bed was empty!

Hugh looked at all the beds. Every one was empty. Then the boy guessed in a flash what was happening.

"It's Mike's birthday and he's having a midnight party somewhere. The beast! He's asked everyone else, and not me! I bet Janet's dormitory is empty too." He slipped out to see. It was as he had guessed – quite empty. All the beds were bare, their coverings turned back. The boy felt angry and hurt. They might have asked him! It was hateful to be left out like this.

"I'm always left out of everything!" he thought, hot tears pricking his eyelids. "Always! Do they think it will make me behave any better to them if they treat me like this! How I hate them! I'll jolly well spoil their feast for them. That will serve them right!"

7

A Shock for the Feasters

Hugh wondered how to spoil the feast.

Should he go and knock on Mr Wills's door and tell him that the dormitories were empty? No – Mr Wills didn't look too kindly on tale-telling. Well, then, he had better find out where the children were feasting and spoil it for them.

He looked out of the window, and by chance he caught sight of a tiny flicker outside. It came from a corner of the big window of the shed. The sack didn't quite cover the glass. Hugh stood and looked at it, wondering where the light came from.

"It's from the big shed," he thought. "So that's where they're feasting. I'll go down and find out!"

Down he went, out of the door, which the children had left open, and into the yard. He went across to the shed, and at once heard the sounds of laughter and whispering inside. He put his eye to the place in the window where the light showed, and saw the scene inside. It was a very merry one.

Empty bottles lay around. Empty tins stood here

and there, and crumbs were all over the place. It was plain that the two dormitories had had a marvellous time. Hugh's heart burned in him. He felt so angry and so miserable that he could almost have gone into the shed and fought every child there!

But he didn't do that. He knew it would be no use. Instead, he took up a large stone and crashed it on to the window! The glass broke at once, with a very loud noise. All the children inside the shed jumped up in fright, their cake falling from their fingers.

"What's that?" said Mike in a panic. "The window is broken. Who did it?"

There was another crash as the second window broke under Hugh's stone. The children were now really afraid. They simply couldn't imagine what was happening.

"The noise will wake everyone up!" cried Mike, in a loud whisper. "Quick, we'd better get back to our dormitories. Leave everything. There isn't time to clear up."

Hugh didn't wait to break the third window. He had seen a light spring up in Mr Wills's room above and he knew the master would be out to see what was happening before another minute had gone by. So he sped lightly up the stairs, and was in his bed before the door of Mr Wills's room opened.

The eleven children opened the door of the shed and fled into the school. They went up the stairs and into the passage where their dormitories were – and just as they were passing Mr Wills's door it opened! Mr Wills stood there in his dressing-gown, staring in amazement at the procession of white-faced children slipping by.

"What are you doing?" he asked. "What was all that noise?"

The children didn't wait to answer. They fled into their rooms and hopped into bed, half dressed as they were, shoes and all. Mr Wills went into the boys' dormitory, switched on the light and looked sternly round. He pulled back the curtains from those cubicles that had them drawn around, and spoke angrily.

"What is the meaning of this? Where have you been? Answer me!"

Nobody answered. The boys were really frightened. Hugh's bed was nearest to Mr Wills, and the master took hold of Hugh's shoulder, shaking him upright.

"You, boy! Answer me! What have you been doing?"

"Sir, I've been in bed all the evening," said Hugh

truthfully. "I don't know what the others have been doing. I wasn't with them."

Mr Wills glared round at the other beds. "I can see that you are half-dressed," he said in an icy voice. "Get out and undress and then get back into bed. I shall want an explanation of this in the morning. You can tell the girls when you see them, that I shall want them too. It seems to me that this is something the heads should know about. Now then – quick – out of bed and undress!"

The boys, all but Hugh, got out of bed and took off their jerseys and other things. Mr Wills told Hugh to get out of bed too.

"But I'm not half-dressed," said Hugh. "I've only got my pyjamas on, sir. I wasn't with the others."

But Mr Wills wasn't believing anyone at all that night. He made Hugh get out too, and saw that he was in his pyjamas as he said. He did not notice one thing – and that was that Hugh had his shoes on! But Mike noticed it.

He was puzzled. Why should Hugh have his shoes on in bed? That was a funny thing to do, surely. And then the boy suddenly guessed the reason.

"Hugh woke up – saw the beds were empty – put on his shoes and slipped down to find us," he thought. "It was he who broke the windows, the beast! He's got us all into this trouble!"

But he said nothing then. He would tell the others in the morning. He slipped back into bed and tried to go to sleep.

All the eleven children were worried when the morning came. They couldn't imagine what Mr Wills was going to do. They soon found out. Mr Wills had gone to the two heads, and it was they that the children were to see, not Mr Wills. This was worse than ever!

"You will go now," said Mr Wills, after prayers were over. "I don't want to hear any explanations from you. You can tell those to the heads. But I may as well tell you that I went down into the shed last night and found the remains of your feast, the candles burning – and the windows smashed. I understand the feast part but why you should smash the windows is beyond me. I am ashamed of you all."

"We didn't smash . . ." began Mike. But Mr Wills wouldn't listen to a word. He waved them all away. Hugh had to go, too, although he kept saying that he hadn't been with the others. Mike had told the others what he suspected about Hugh, and every boy and girl looked at him with disgust and dislike.

They went to see the heads. Their knees shook, and Emily began to cry. Even Janet felt the tears coming. All the children were tired, and some of them had eaten too much and didn't feel well.

The heads looked stern. They asked a few questions, and then made Tom tell the whole story.

"I can understand your wanting to have some sort of a party on Michael's birthday," said Miss Lesley, "but to end it by smashing windows is disgusting behaviour. It shows a great lack of self-control."

"I think it was Hugh who broke the windows," said Mike, not able to keep it back any longer. "We wouldn't have done that, Miss Lesley. For one thing we would have been afraid of being caught if we did that – it made such a noise. But, you see, we left Hugh out of the party and I think that out of spite he smashed the windows to give us a shock, and to make sure we would be caught."

"Did you do that, Hugh?" asked the headmaster, looking at the red-faced boy.

"No, sir," said Hugh, in a low voice. "I was in bed asleep. I don't know anything about it."

"Well, then, why was it you had your shoes on in bed when Mr Wills made you get out last night?" burst out Tom. "Mike saw them!"

Hugh said nothing, but looked obstinate. He meant to stick to his story, no matter what was said.

The punishment was very just. "As you have missed almost a night's sleep, you will all go to bed an hour earlier for a week," said Miss Lesley.

"And you will please pay for the mending of the windows," said the headmaster. "You too, Hugh. I am not going to go into the matter of how the windows got broken – but I think Michael is speaking the truth when he says that he would not have thought of smashing windows because of the noise. All the same, you will all twelve of you share for the mending of the windows. I will deduct it from your pocket-money."

"And please remember, children, that although it is good to have fun, you are sent here to work and to learn things that will help you to earn your living later on," said Miss Lesley. "There are some of you here working for scholarships, and you will not be able to win them if you behave like this."

The children went out, feeling very miserable. It was hateful to go to bed early – earlier even than the first-formers. And they felt bitter about the payment for the windows, because they themselves had not broken them.

"Though if we hadn't held the feast, the windows wouldn't have been broken," said Mike. "So in a way it was because of us they got smashed. But I know it was Hugh who did it, out of spite. Let's not say a word to him. Let's send him to Coventry and be as beastly as we can."

So Hugh had a very bad time. He was snubbed by the whole of his class. The first- and third-formers joined in too, and nobody ever spoke a word to him, unless it was a whispered, "Sneak! Tell-tale! Sneak!" which made him feel worse than if he had not been spoken to.

He worried very much over the whole thing. It was awful to have no friends, terrible to be treated so badly. He knew it was stupid and wrong to have broken the windows like that. He had done it in a fit of spiteful temper, and now it couldn't be undone.

He couldn't sleep at night. He rose the next day looking white and tired. He couldn't do his work, and the teachers scolded him, for he was one of the children who were going in for the scholarship. He couldn't remember what he had learned, and although he spent hours doing his prep, he got poor marks for it.

Hugh knew that he must win the scholarship, for his parents were not well-off and needed help with his schooling. He had brothers and a sister who were very clever, and who had won many scholarships between them. Hugh didn't want to let his family down. He mustn't be the only one who couldn't do anything.

"The worst of it is, I haven't got good brains, as they have," thought the boy, as he tried to learn a list of history dates. "Everything is hard to me. It's easy to them. Dad and Mum don't realise that. They think I must be as clever as the rest of the family, and I'm not. So they get angry with me when I'm not top of my form, though, goodness knows, I swot hard enough and try to be."

The children all paid between them for the windows. They were mended and the remains of the feast were cleared away. The week went by, and the period for early going to bed passed by too. The children began to forget about the feast and its unfortunate ending. But they didn't forget their dislike for Hugh.

"I shan't speak a word to him for the rest of the term," said Peter. And the others said the same. Only Janet felt sorry for the boy, and noticed how white and miserable he looked. But she had to be loyal to the others, and so she said nothing to him too, and looked away whenever he came near.

"I can't stick this!" Hugh thought to himself. "I simply can't. I wish I could run away! I wish I was old enough to join a ship and go to sea. I hate school!"

8

A Shock for Tom – and for Hugh

The days slipped by, and each one was full of interest. Janet and Mike liked their work, and loved their play. They loved being friends with Tom, and they liked all the others in their form, except Hugh.

The great excitement now was craftwork. The boys were doing carpentry, and the things they were making were really beginning to take shape. The girls were doing raffia-work and were weaving some really lovely baskets. Janet couldn't help gloating over the basket she was making. It was a big work-basket for her mother, in every bright colour Janet could use. Mike was making a very fine letter-rack for his father.

But the best thing of all that was being made in the carpentry class was Tom's. The boy was mad on ships, and he had made a beautiful model. He was now doing the rigging, and the slender masts were beginning to look very good indeed, set with snowy sails and fine thread instead of ropes.

There were wide windowsills in the craftwork

and carpentry room, and on these the children set out their work, so that any other form could see what they were doing. They all took a deep interest in what the others were making. Tom's ship was greatly admired and the boy was really very proud of it.

"I think this is the only class you really work in, Tom, isn't it?" the woodwork master said, bending over Tom's model. "My word, if you worked half as hard in the other classes as you do in mine, you would certainly never be bottom. You're an intelligent boy – yes, very intelligent – and you can use your brains well when you want to."

Tom flushed with pleasure. He gazed at his beautiful ship and his heart swelled with pride as he thought of how it would look on his mantelpiece at home, when it was quite finished. It was almost finished now – he was soon going to paint it. He hoped there would be time to begin the painting that afternoon.

But there wasn't. "Put your things away," said the master. "Hurry, Peter. You mustn't be late for your next class."

The children cleared up, and put their models on the wide windowsills. The master opened the windows to let in fresh air, and then gave the order to file out to the children's own classroom, two floors below. The craftwork rooms were at the top of the school, lovely big, light rooms with plenty of sun and air.

The next lesson was geography. Miss Thomas wanted a map that was not in the corner and told Hugh to go and get it from one of the cupboards on the top landing. The children stood up to answer questions while Hugh was gone.

In the middle of the questions, something curious happened. A whitish object suddenly fell quickly past the schoolroom windows and landed with a dull thud on the stone path by the bed. The children looked round in interest. What could it have been? Not a bird, surely?

Mike was next to the window. He peeped out to see what it was – and then he gave a cry of dismay.

"What's the matter?" asked the teacher, startled.

"Oh, Miss Thomas, it looks as if Tom's lovely ship is lying broken on the path outside," said Mike. Tom darted to the window. He gave a wail of dismay.

"It is my ship. Somebody has pushed it off the windowsill, and it's smashed. All the rigging is spoiled! The masts are broken!"

The boy's voice trembled, for he had really loved his ship. He had spent so many hours making it. It had been very nearly perfect.

There was a silence in the room. Everyone was shocked, and felt very sorry for Tom. In the middle of the silence the door opened and Hugh came in, carrying the map.

At once the same thought flashed into everyone's mind. Hugh had been to the top of the school to get the map – the cupboard was opposite the woodwork room – and Hugh had slipped in and pushed Tom's ship out of the window to smash it!

"You did it!" shouted Mike. Hugh looked astonished.

"Did what?" he asked.

"Smashed Tom's ship!" cried half a dozen voices.

"I don't know what you're talking about," said Hugh, really puzzled.

"That will do," said Miss Thomas. "Tom, go and collect your ship. It may not be so badly damaged as you think. Hugh, sit down. Do you know anything about the ship?"

"Not a thing," said Hugh. "The door of the woodwork room was shut when I went to get the map."

"Story-teller!" whispered half a dozen children.

"Silence!" rapped out Miss Thomas. She was worried. She knew that Tom had been hated by Hugh ever since last term, and she feared that the boy really had smashed up the ship. She made up her mind to find out about it from Hugh himself, after the lesson. She felt sure she would know if the boy were telling her the truth or not, once she really began to question him.

But it was not Miss Thomas that Hugh feared. It was the children! As soon as morning school was over they surrounded him and accused him bitterly, calling him every name they could think of.

"I didn't do it, I didn't do it," said Hugh, pushing away the hands that held him. "Don't pin everything on to me simply because I've done one or two mean things. I didn't do that. I liked Tom's ship, too."

But nobody believed him. They gave the boy a very bad time and by the time that six o'clock came, Hugh was so battered by the children's looks and tongues that he crept up to his dormitory to be by himself. Then the tears came and he sobbed to himself, ashamed because he could not stop.

"I'm going away," he said. "I can't stay here now. I'm going home. Dad and Mum will be angry with me, but I won't come back here. I can't do anything right. I didn't smash that lovely ship. I liked it just as much as the others did."

He began to stuff some of his clothes into a

small case. He hardly knew what he was doing. He knew there was a train at a quarter to seven. He would catch that.

The other children wondered where he was. "Good thing for him he's not here," said Peter. "I've thought of a few more names to call him, the horrid beast!"

They were all in their common-room, discussing the affair. Tom's ship stood on the mantelpiece, looking very sorry for itself. The woodwork master came to see it.

"It's not as bad as it might be," he said cheerfully. "Just a bit dented here. Those masts can easily be renewed, and you can do the rigging again. You're good at that. Cheer up, Tom!"

The master went out. "All very well for him to talk like that," said Tom gloomily. "But it isn't his ship. I don't feel the same about it now it's spoiled."

There came a knock at the common-room door. It was such a timid, faint knock that at first none of the children heard it. Then it came again, a little louder.

"There's someone knocking at the door," said Angie, in astonishment, for no one ever knocked at their door.

"Come in!" yelled the whole form. The door opened and a first-former looked in. It was a small boy, with a very white, scared face.

"Hello, Paul. What's up?" said Fred.

"I w-w-w-want to speak to T-T-T-Tom," stammered the small boy, whose knees were knocking together in fright.

"Well, here I am," said Tom. "Don't look so scared. I shan't eat you!"

The small boy opened and shut his mouth like a fish, but not another word came out. The children began to giggle.

"Paul, whatever's the matter?" cried Janet. "Has somebody frightened you?"

"N-n-n-no," stammered Paul. "I want to tell Tom something. But I'm afraid to."

"What is it?" asked Tom kindly. He was always kind to the younger ones, and they all liked him. "What have you been doing? Breaking windows or something?"

"No, Tom, m-m-m-much worse than that," said the boy, looking at Tom with big, scared eyes. "It's – it's about your lovely ship. That ship there," and he pointed to the mantelpiece.

"Well, what about it?" said Tom, thinking that Paul was going to tell him how he had seen Hugh push it out of the window.

"Oh, Tom, it was my fault it got broken!" wailed the little boy, breaking into loud sobs. "I was in the woodwork room with Dick Dennison, and we were fooling about. And I fell against the windowsill and – and – "

"Go on," said Tom.

"I put out my hand to save myself," sobbed Paul, "and it struck your lovely ship – and sent it toppling out of the open window. I was so frightened, Tom."

There was a long silence after this speech. So Hugh hadn't anything to do with the ship, after all! No wonder he had denied it so vigorously. All the children stared at the white-faced Paul.

"I d-d-d-didn't dare to tell anyone," went on the small boy. "Dick swore he wouldn't tell either. But then we heard that you had accused Hugh of doing it and we knew we couldn't do anything but come and own up. So I came because it was me that pushed it out – quite by accident, Tom."

"I see," said Tom slowly. He looked at the scared boy and gave him a kindly push. "All right. Don't worry. You did right to come and tell me. Come straight away another time you do anything, old son – you see, we've done an injustice to somebody else and that's not good. Go along back to your common-room. I daresay I can manage to mend the ship all right."

The small boy gave Tom a grateful look out of tearful eyes, and shot out of the room at top speed. He tore back to his common-room, feeling as if a great load had been taken off his heart.

When he had gone, the children looked at one another. "Well, it wasn't Hugh after all," said Janet, saying what everyone else was thinking.

"No," said Tom. "It wasn't. And I called him a good many beastly names. For once they were unjust. And I hate injustice."

Everyone felt uncomfortable. "Well, anyway, he's done things just as horrid," said Peter. "It's no wonder we thought it was him. Especially as he just happened to be by the woodwork room at the time."

"Yes," said Mike. "That was unlucky for him. What are we going to do about it?"

Nobody said anything. Nobody wanted to apologise to Hugh. Tom stared out of the window.

"We've got to do something," he said. "Where is he? We'd better find him and get him here, and then tell him we made a mistake. We were ready enough to be beastly — now we must be ready to be sorry."

"I'll go and find him," said Janet. She had remembered Hugh's startled face as the others had suddenly accused him when he had come into the room carrying the map. She thought, too, of his miserable look when they had all pressed round him after tea, calling him horrid names. They had been unjust. Hugh had done many mean things — but not that one. Janet suddenly wanted to say she was sorry.

She sped into the classroom. Hugh wasn't there. She ran to the gym. He wasn't there either. She looked into each music room, and in the library, where Hugh often went to choose books. But he was nowhere to be found.

"Where can he be?" thought the little girl. "He can't be out. His clothes are hanging up. What has he done with himself?"

She thought of the dormitory. She ran up the stairs and met Hugh just coming out, carrying a bag, with the marks of tears still on his face. She ran up to him.

"Hugh! Where have you been? What are you doing with that bag? Listen, we want you to come downstairs."

"No, you don't," said Hugh. "None of you want me. I'm going home."

"Hugh! What do you mean?" cried Janet, in alarm. "Oh, Hugh, listen. We know who broke Tom's ship. It was little Paul. He pushed it out of the window by accident! Don't go home, Hugh. Come down and hear what we have to say!"

9

Things are Cleared Up!

But Hugh pushed past Janet roughly. He did not mean to change his mind. Janet was scared. It seemed a dreadful thing to her that Hugh should run away because of the unkindness he had received from his class. She caught hold of the boy and tried to pull him back into the dormitory.

"Don't," said Hugh. "Let me go. You're just as bad as the others, Janet. It's no good you trying to stop me now."

"Oh, do listen to me, Hugh," said Janet. "Just listen for half a minute. Paul came and owned up about the ship. He pushed it out of the window when he was fooling about. And now you can't think how sorry we are that we accused you."

Hugh went back into the dormitory, and sat on the bed. "Well," he said bitterly, "you may feel pretty awful about it – but just think how I must feel always to have you thinking horrid things about me, and calling me names, and turning away when you meet me. And think how I felt when I woke up the other night and found everyone had gone to a midnight feast – except me! You've never been left out of anything. Everyone likes you. You don't know what it's like to be miserable."

Janet took Hugh's cold hand. She was very troubled. "Hugh," she said, "we did mean to ask you to our feast. Mike and Tom and I planned that we would. We didn't want you to be left out."

"Well, why didn't you ask me then?" demanded Hugh. "It would have made all the difference in the world to me if only you had. I'd have felt terribly happy. As it was you made me lose my temper and do something horrid and spiteful. I've been ashamed of it ever since. I spoiled your feast – and got you all into trouble. I wanted to do that, I know, but all the same I've been ashamed. And now that I'm going to run away, I want you to tell the others something for me."

"What?" asked Janet, almost in tears.

"Tell them I did break the windows, of course," said Hugh, "and tell them that I want to pay for them. They had to pay a share – well, give them this money and let them share it out between them. I wanted to do that before, only I kept saying I hadn't broken the windows, so I couldn't very well offer to pay, could I? But now I can."

Hugh took some money out of his pocket. He

counted it and gave it to Janet. "There you are," he said. "I can't do much to put right what I did, but I can at least do this. Now goodbye, Janet, I'm going."

"No, don't go, Hugh, please don't," said Janet, her voice trembling. "Please come down and let us all tell you we're sorry. Don't go."

But Hugh shook off her hand and went quickly down the stairs, carrying his little bag. Janet flew down to the common-room, tears in her eyes and the money in her hand. She burst in at the door, and everyone turned to see what she had to say.

"I found him," said Janet. "He's – he's running away. Isn't it dreadful? He says he's ashamed of himself now for breaking the windows, and he's given me that money to give you, to pay for the whole amount. And oh Mike, oh Tom, somehow I can understand now why he broke those windows – he was so miserable at being left out!"

"I do wish we hadn't accused him unjustly," began Peter. "It's an awful pity he cheated last term like that. He seemed quite a decent chap till then – but somehow we got it into our heads after that that he was a dreadful boy and we didn't really give him a chance."

"Look here – I'm going after him," said Tom suddenly. "If the heads get to know about this, we'll all get into awful trouble, and goodness knows what will happen to Hugh. What's the time? Half past six? I can catch him then, before he gets on the train."

He ran out of the school building and went to the shed where Mr Wills's bicycle was kept. He wheeled it out and jumped on it. Down the drive he went and out of the great school gates.

He pedalled fast, for it was quite a way to the station. He kept his eyes open for Hugh, but it was not until he had almost come to the station that he saw the boy. Hugh was running fast. He had been running all the way, because he had been so afraid of missing the train.

Tom rode up close to him, jumped off the bicycle, clutched Hugh's arm and pulled him to the side of the road. He threw the bicycle against the hedge, and then dragged the astonished boy into a nearby field.

"What's up? Oh, it's you, Tom! Let me go. I'm going home."

"No, you're not," said Tom. "Not until you hear what I've got to say, anyway. Listen. Hugh. We're ashamed of ourselves. We really are. It's true you've been pretty beastly and spiteful – but it was partly because of us. I mean, we made you behave like that. I see that now. If we'd behaved differently you might have, too. You were a decent chap till the end of last term. We all liked you."

"I know," said Hugh, in a low voice. "I was happy till then. Then I cheated. I know there's no excuse for cheating – but I had a reason for my cheating. It seemed a good reason to me then, but I see it wasn't now. Somehow or other I had to pass that exam," said Hugh. "All my brothers and my sister are clever and pass exams and win scholarships, and my father said I mustn't let the family down. I must pass mine too. Well, I'm not really clever. That is why I have to swot so hard, and never have time to play and go for walks as the rest of you do. So, as I was afraid I'd not pass the exam, I cheated a bit. And you gave me away."

"I didn't," said Tom. "I saw you'd cheated, but I didn't give you away. Why don't you believe that? Miss Thomas found it out."

"Do you swear you didn't give me away?" said Hugh.

"I swear I didn't!" said Tom. "You've never known me to sneak, have you, or to tell lies? I do a lot of silly things and play the fool, but I don't do mean things."

"All right. I believe you," said Hugh. "But I can't tell you how the thought of that cheating, and knowing that you all knew it, weighed on my mind. You see, I'm not really a cheat."

"I see," said Tom. "It's really your parents' fault for trying to drive you too hard. You're silly. You should tell them."

"I'm going to," said Hugh. "That's one thing I'm going home to say now. And I've been so miserable this term that what brains I have won't work at all! So it's no good me trying for the scholarship anyhow. Somehow things aren't fair. There's you with brains, and you don't bother to use them. There's clever Janet and Mike, and they fool about and don't really try to be top when they could. And there's me, with poor brains, doing my very best and getting nowhere."

Tom suddenly felt terribly ashamed of all his fooling and playing. He felt ashamed of making Mike and Janet do bad work too, for they none of them really tried their hardest. He bit his lip and stared into the darkness.

"I've done as much wrong as you have," he said at last. "You cheated because you hadn't got good enough brains – and I've wasted my good brains and not used them. So I've cheated too, in another way. I never thought of it like that before. Hugh, come back with me. Let's start again. It's all been a stupid mistake. Look – give us a chance to show you we're sorry, won't you?"

"You didn't give me a chance," said Hugh.

"I know. So you can feel awfully generous if you will give us a chance!" said Tom. "And look here, old son, I'm not going to waste my good brains any more and cheat the teachers out of what I could really do if I tried – I'm going to work hard. I'll help you, if you'll help me. I don't know how to work hard, but you can show me – and I'll help you with my brains. See?"

Just then a loud whistle came from the station and then a train pulled out. Hugh looked at the train.

"Well, the train's gone," he said. "So I can't go with it. I'll have to come back with you. Let me sleep over it and see how I feel in the morning. I don't want to see any of you again tonight. I should feel awkward. If I make up my mind I can begin all over again I'll nod at you when we get up – and just let's all act as if nothing had happened. I can't stand any more of this sort of thing. I simply must work if I'm going to enter for that scholarship."

"Good chap," said Tom, collecting Mr Wills's bicycle from the hedge where he had thrown it. "Come on, then."

The two boys went back together. Hugh went straight upstairs to his dormitory, telling Tom to

say that he didn't want any supper. But before he went, Hugh held out his hand.

There was a warm handshake between the two of them and then Tom went soberly back to the common-room, wondering what to say. The children crowded round him and Tom explained what had happened.

When they heard what Hugh had said about how he was expected to do as well as his brothers and sister, and how he knew he hadn't good enough brains, they were silent. They knew then why Hugh had swotted so much. They even understood why he had been tempted to cheat. Every child knew how horrid it was to disappoint parents or let their family down.

"Well, let's hope he'll make up his mind to stay," said Tom. "And listen, I feel quite a bit ashamed of my behaviour too. My parents pay for me to learn things here, and I never try at all – except in woodwork. I just fool about the whole time, and make you laugh. Well, from now on, I'm going to do a spot of work. And so are you, Mike and Janet. You've neither of you been top once this term, and you could easily be near it, and give Delia a shock!"

"All right," said Janet, who had been thinking quite a lot too, that night. "I'll work. Miss Thomas said today she would give me a bad report because I've not been doing my best. I don't want that. Mike will work too. We always do the same."

Hugh was asleep when the children went up to bed. For the first night for a long time he was at peace, and slept calmly without worrying. Things had been cleared up. He was happier.

In the morning the boys got up when the bell went. Tom heard Hugh whistling softly to himself as he dressed, and he was glad. Then a head was put round Tom's curtains, and Tom saw Hugh's face. It was all smiles, and looked quite different from usual.

Tom stared at the smiling head. It nodded violently up and down and disappeared. Tom felt glad. Hugh was doing the sensible thing – starting all over again, and giving the others a chance to do the same thing!

What a change there was for Hugh that morning when the boys and girls met in their common-room! He was one of them now, not an outcast, and everyone felt much happier because of it.

10

End of Term

Miss Thomas and the other teachers had a pleasant shock that week. For the first time since he had been at St Rollo's Tom began to work! The teachers simply couldn't understand it. Not only Tom worked, though – Mike and Janet did too.

"Something's happened that we don't know about," said Miss Thomas to Mr Wills. "And do you notice how much happier that boy Hugh looks? It seems as if the others have decided to be nicer to him. It's funny how Tom seems to have made friends with him all of a sudden. They even seem to be working together!"

So they were. They did their prep together, and learned many things from each other. Tom's quick brains were useful at understanding many things that Hugh's slow brains did not take in – and Hugh's ability for really getting down to things, once he understood them, was a fine example for the rather lazy Tom.

"You make a good team," said Miss Thomas approvingly. "I am pleased with you both. Tom, I think it would be a good idea to move you away from that front desk, and put you beside Hugh. You can help one another quite a lot."

"Oooh, good," said Tom, his eyes gleaming. "It does rather cramp my style, Miss Thomas, to be under your eye all the time, you know."

The class laughed. They had been surprised at Tom's sudden change of mind regarding his work. But they were afraid that he might no longer fool about as he used to do. He always caused so much amusement – it would be sad if he no longer thought of his amazing tricks.

"Don't worry," said Tom, when Mike told him this. "I shall break out at times. I can't stop thinking of tricks even if I'm using my brains for my work too!"

He kept his word, and played one or two laughable tricks on poor Monsieur Crozier, nearly driving him mad. Tom provided him with a pen on his desk which, on being pressed for writing, sent out a stream of water from its end. The French master was so angry that he threw the blackboard chalk down on the floor and stamped on it.

This amused the class immensely, and was talked of for a long time. In fact, that term, on the whole, was a very exciting one indeed. Mike and Janet got quite a shock when they realised that the holidays would begin in a week's time!

"Oh! Fancy the term being so nearly over!" said Janet dolefully.

"Gracious, Janet, don't you want to be home for Christmas?" said Marian.

"Yes, of course," said Janet. "But it's such fun being at St Rollo's. Think of the things that have happened this term!"

Miss Thomas overheard her. She smiled. "Shall I tell you what is the most surprising thing that has happened?" she said.

"What?" asked the children, crowding round. Miss Thomas held the list of marks for the last week in her hand. She held it up.

"Well, for the first time this term Tom Young isn't bottom!" she said. "I couldn't believe my eyes when I added up the marks – in fact I added them all up again to make sure. And it's true – he actually isn't bottom. Really, the world must be coming to an end!"

Everyone roared with laughter. Tom went red. He was pleased.

"I suppose I'm next to bottom, though," he said, with a twinkle.

"Not even that!" said Miss Thomas. "You are sixth from the top – simply amazing. And Hugh has gone up too – he is seventh. And as for Mike and Janet – well, wonders will never cease! They tie for second place, only two marks behind Delia!"

Mike, Janet, Tom and Hugh were delighted. It really was nice to find that good work so soon showed results. Hugh took Tom's arm.

"I can't tell you how you've helped me," he said. "Not only in my work – in other ways too. I feel quite different."

The children thought that Hugh looked different too. He smiled and laughed and joked with the others, and went for walks as they did. Who would have thought that things could possibly have turned out like that, after all?

The term came quickly to an end. There were concerts and craftwork exhibitions – and, not quite so pleasant, exams as well! All the children became excited at the thought of Christmas, pantomimes, presents and parties, and the teachers had to make allowances for very high spirits.

The last day came. There was a terrific noise everywhere, as packing went on in each dormitory, and boys and girls rushed up and down the stairs, looking for pencil-boxes, books, boots, shoes and other things. There were collisions everywhere, and squeals of laughter as things rolled down the stairs with a clatter.

"I suppose all this noise is necessary," sighed Mr

Wills, stepping aside to avoid somebody's football, which was bouncing down the stairs all by itself, accompanied above by a gale of laughter. "Dear me – how glad I shall be to say goodbye to all you hooligans! What a pity to think you are coming back next term!"

"Oh no, sir, we're glad!" shouted Mike, rushing down after the football. "We'll love the holidays but it will be grand to come back to St Rollo's!"

Goodbyes were said all round. Some of the children were going home by train, some by car.

"Good!" said Janet. "We don't need to say goodbye till we get to London. Look – there's our coach at the door. Come on!"

They piled into the big coach with about twenty other children. It set off for the station. The children looked back at the big grey building.

"Goodbye St Rollo's," said Mike. "See you next term. Goodbye! Goodbye!"

THE CHILDREN
OF KIDILLIN

1

The Meeting of the Four Cousins

One day in 1940, two children and a dog raced down to a village sweet-shop in excitement. They opened the little door of Mrs MacPherson's shop and went inside.

"Good morning," said Mrs MacPherson, in her soft Scottish voice. "You looked excited, the two of you."

"We are," said Sandy, a tall boy with a jolly, freckled face. "We've got our English cousins coming to live with us till the war's over! We've never even seen them!"

"They're about the same age as we are," said Jeanie, Sandy's sister. "One's called Tom, and the other's called Sheila. They live in London, but their parents want them to go somewhere safe till the war's over. They're coming tomorrow!"

"So we've come down to get some of your bull's-eye peppermints for them," said Sandy.

"And will they do lessons with Miss Mitchell, your governess?" asked Mrs MacPherson, getting down her big jar of peppermint humbugs. "It will be right nice company for you. It's to be hoped the town children don't find it dull down here," she added, handing over a fat bag of sweets. Sandy and Jeanie stared at her in surprise.

"Dull!" said Jeanie, quite crossly. "How could anyone find Kidillin dull? There's the river that rushes through Kidillin, and the hills around, and away yonder the sea!"

"Ay, but there's no cinema for twelve miles, and only three shops, not a train for ten miles, and no buses!" said Mrs MacPherson. "And what will town children do without those, I should like to know?"

The two children left the little shop. They gazed into the two other shops of Kidillin, which were general stores and sold most things, and then made their way home again, each sucking a peppermint.

Sandy and Jeanie were really indignant at the thought that anyone could be bored with Kidillin. They loved their quiet Scottish life, they loved Kidillin House, their home, and enjoyed their lessons with Miss Mitchell, their old governess. They knew every inch of the hills about their home, they knew the flowers that grew there, the birds and the animals that lived there, and every cottager within miles.

Sandy and Jeanie were to drive to the nearest town to meet their cousins the next day. So, with Miss Mitchell driving the horse, they set off. It was a long way, but the autumn day was bright and sunny, and the mountains that rose up around were beautiful. The children sang as they went, and the clip-clop of the horse's feet was a pleasant sound to hear.

The train came in as they arrived at the station. Sandy and Jeanie almost fell out of the trap as they heard its whistle. They rushed through the little gate and on to the platform.

And there stood a boy and a girl, with a pile of luggage around them – and a dog on a lead!

"Hello!" cried Sandy. "Are you Tom and Sheila?"

"Yes," said the boy. "I suppose you are Sandy and Jeanie. This is our dog, Paddy. We hope you don't mind us bringing him – but we couldn't, we really couldn't leave him behind!"

"Well, I hope he gets on all right with our dog," said Sandy doubtfully. "Mack is rather a jealous sort of dog. Come on. We've got the trap outside. The porter will bring out your luggage."

The four children, the dog, and a porter, went out to Miss Mitchell. She shook hands with Tom and Sheila, thought that Sheila was very pretty, but far too pale, and that Tom was too tall for his age. But they had nice manners, and she liked the look of them.

"Welcome to Scotland, my new pupils!" said Miss Mitchell. "Get in – dear me, is that your dog? I hope he won't fight Mack."

It looked very much as if Paddy would certainly fight Mack! The two dogs growled, bared their teeth and strained hard at their leads. Their hair rose on their necks and they looked most ferocious.

"What an unfriendly dog Mack is," said Tom. This was not at all the right thing to say. Sandy looked angry.

"You mean, what an unfriendly dog your Paddy

is," he said. "Our Mack would have been pleased enough to see him if he hadn't growled like that."

"Mack can come up on the front seat with me," said Miss Mitchell hastily. She didn't want the cousins to quarrel within the first five minutes of their meeting.

"Then I shall drive," said Sandy at once. He wasn't going to sit behind in the trap and talk politely to a boy who was rude about Mack.

"Can you drive this trap yourself?" said Sheila in surprise.

"Of course," said Sandy. "I've driven it since I was four." He thought Sheila was rather a nice girl – but Jeanie didn't! Jeanie thought Sheila was too dressed-up for anything!

"How does she think she's going to walk on the hills in those shoes?" thought Jeanie scornfully, looking at Sheila's pretty button-shoes. "And what a fussy dress! All frills and ribbons! But I like Tom. He's nice and tall."

They drove home. Miss Mitchell did most of the talking, and asked the two London children all about the home they had left. They answered politely, looking round at the countryside all the time.

"Doesn't it all look awfully big, Sheila," said Tom. "Look at those mountains! Oh – what a funny little village! What is it called?"

"It is Kidillin," said Jeanie. "We live not far away, at Kidillin House. Look – you can see it above those trees there."

Sheila and Tom looked at the plain, rather ugly stone house set on the hillside. They did not like the look of it at all. When they had gone to stay with their uncle in the English countryside the year before, they had lived in a lovely old thatched cottage, cosy and friendly – but this old stone house looked so cold and stern.

"I hope the war will soon be over!" said Tom, who really meant that he hoped he wouldn't have to stay very long at Kidillin. Sandy and Jeanie knew quite well what he was really thinking, and they were hurt and angry.

"They are as unfriendly as their dog!" whispered Jeanie to Sandy, as they jumped down from the cart. "I'm not going to like them a bit."

"I wish we were at home!" whispered Sheila to Tom, as they went up the steps to the front door. "It's going to be horrid, being here!"

2

The Old Cottage on the Hillside

For the first few days things were very difficult for all four children, and for the two dogs as well. They were even more difficult for poor Miss Mitchell! Sandy and Jeanie never quarrelled – but now she had four children who bickered and squabbled all day long!

As for the dogs, they had to be kept well apart, for they each seemed to wish to tear the other to pieces! They had to take it in turns to be tied up so that they could not fly at one another all day long.

"And really, I'm wishing I could tie up the children too," Miss Mitchell said to Sandy's mother. "For they're like the dogs – just ready to fly at one another's throats all day long!"

Mrs MacLaren laughed. "Give them time to settle down to each other," she said. "And you'd better begin lessons again tomorrow, Miss Mitchell – that will keep them out of mischief a bit."

Sandy and Jeanie had been showing off to Tom and Sheila. They had taken them for a long walk, up a difficult mountain, where a good deal of rough climbing had to be done. The English children had panted and puffed, and poor Sheila's shoes were no use at all for such walking.

"Can't we have a rest again?" asked Sheila at last. "I'm so tired. This is a dreadful place for walking. I'd much rather walk in the park!"

"In the park!" said Sandy scornfully. "What, when there's fine country like this, and soft heather to your feet! And look at the view there – you can see the sea!"

The four children sat down. Far away they could see the blue glimmer of the sea, and could hear very faintly the shrill cry of the circling gulls. Tom was so tired that he only gave the view a moment's look, and then lay down on his back. "Phew, I'm tired!" he said. "I vote we go back."

"But we're not yet at the burn we want to show you," said Jeanie. Sheila giggled.

"It does sound so funny for a stream to be called a burn!" she said. "It sounds as if something was on fire – going to see the burn!"

"The bur-r-r-rn, not the burn," said Sandy, sounding the r in burn. "Can't you talk properly?"

"We can talk just as well as you!" said Tom, vexed, and then off they went, squabbling again!

Mack, who was with the children, barked when he heard them quarrelling. He wanted someone to quarrel with too! But Paddy was at home, tied up, much to Tom's annoyance.

"Be quiet," said Tom to Mack. "I can't hear myself speak when you begin that noise. Where are you going, Sandy? I want to rest a bit more."

"There'll be no time to finish the walk if you lie there any longer," said Sandy. "This is the fourth time we've stopped for you – a lazy lot of folk you Londoners must be!"

"All right. Then we'll be lazy!" said Tom angrily. "You and Jeanie go on, and Sheila and I will stay here till you come back – and you can go and find your wonderful bur-r-r-r-rn yourself!"

"Oh, do come, Tom," begged Jeanie. "It really is a strange sight to see. The water comes pouring out a hole in the hillside – just as if somebody had turned a tap on!"

"Well, don't you go rushing up the mountain so quickly then," said Tom, getting up. "I'm sure you're just showing off! I bet you and Sandy don't go so fast when you're alone! You're just trying to make us feel silly."

Jeanie went red. It was quite true – she and Sandy had planned together to take the two Londoners for a stiff walk up the mountains, going at a fast pace, just to show them what Scots children could do. And now Tom had guessed what she and Sandy had planned.

"Oh come on," said Sandy impatiently. They all went up the steep, heathery slope, rounded a big crag, and then slipped and slid on a stony stretch that scratched Sheila's shoes to bits!

Suddenly there was a rumble of thunder round the mountain. Tom looked up anxiously. "I say! Is there going to be a storm?" he said. "Sheila always gets a cold if she gets soaked. Is there anywhere to shelter?"

"There's an old tumbledown hut not far from here," said Sandy. "Come on – run!"

The rain began to fall. The four children and the dog ran full-pelt over the heather, up another slope, round a group of wind-blown pine trees – and there, in front of them, tucked into the mountainside, was an old, tumbledown cottage!

The children rushed to the door, flung it open and ran inside. They shook themselves like dogs, and the rain flew off their clothes, just as it was flying off Mack's coat. Then Sandy gave a cry of surprise. "I say! Somebody lives here! Look!"

The children looked around the little stone house. It was roughly furnished with chairs, a table and two camp beds. An oil-stove stood in a corner, and something was cooking on it.

"Funny!" said Jeanie, staring round. "Nobody's

here at all — and yet there's something cooking on the stove."

"Perhaps there's someone in the tiny room at the back," said Sandy, and he pushed open the door and looked inside. The boy stopped in the greatest surprise. Nobody was there — nobody at all — but the whole room seemed full of a strange-looking machine, that had knobs and handles, valves and levers on it. Sandy was just going to tell Tom to come and see when he heard footsteps.

He shut the door of the little room quickly, just as the door of the house swung open, and a fat man came in. He was so astonished when he saw the children that he couldn't say a word. He stood and gaped at them in amazement. Then he turned a purple-red and caught Tom by the shoulder.

He made peculiar noises, and pushed the boy out of the door so roughly that he almost fell. He was just about to do the same to Jeanie when Sandy stepped up and stopped him. The boy stood there in his kilt, glowering at the angry man.

"Don't you dare touch my sister!" he said. "What's up with you? There was a storm coming on, and we came in here out of the rain. We didn't know anyone lived here — it's always been empty before. We'll go if you don't want to give us shelter!"

There was the sound of footsteps again and another man came into the house, looking dismayed and astonished. He began to roar at the children.

"What are you doing here? Clear out! If you come here again I'll set my dog on you!"

The children stumbled out of the old hut in a fright. The second man caught hold of Tom and shook him. "Did you go into the room at the back?" he demanded. "Did you? Go on, answer me! If you've come to steal anything, you'll be sorry."

"Of course we haven't come to steal anything!" said Tom indignantly. "No, I didn't go into any room at all except the one you found us in — I didn't even know there was another room! So keep your silly secrets to yourself!"

The man made as if he would rush at him, but Mack somehow got in between, and tripped the man over. He sat up nursing his ankle, looking as black as thunder.

"Loose the dog, Carl!" he yelled. "Loose the dog."

"Come on," said Sandy at once. "It's a big brute of a dog. I can see it over there. It would eat Mack up!"

The four children flew down the path in the

rain. No dog came after them. The rain poured down, and Tom looked anxiously at Sheila again. "We really shall have to shelter somewhere," he said, "Sheila is getting soaked and I promised Mother I'd look after her."

"There's an overhanging rock by the burn we wanted to show you," said Sandy stopping. "But it's rather near that old hut. Still, the men won't see us there, and they'll think we've gone home frightened, anyway. Come on!"

Sandy led the way. In a few minutes they came within the sound of rushing water, and then Tom saw a great craggy rock. They went towards it, and were soon crouching under it out of the rain.

"This is the burn, or stream, we wanted to show you," said Sandy. "Look – it gushes out of the hole in this rock. Isn't it strange? It comes from the heart of the mountain – we always think it's very strange."

It *was* strange. There was a large, uneven hole in one side of the great rock, and from it poured a clear stream of water that fell down the mountainside in a little gully it had made for itself. On and on it went down the mountain until, near the bottom, it joined the rushing River Spelter.

"Jeanie and I have climbed down beside this water all the way from this stone to the river," said

Sandy proudly. "It's very difficult to do that. We had to take a rope with us to get down at some places, because the burn becomes a waterfall at times!"

Tom was very interested in the torrent that poured out of the hole in the rock. He went close up to it and peered into the hole, whose mouth was almost hidden by the spate of water.

"Does this water get less when there are no rains?" he asked. Sandy nodded.

"Yes," he said, "it's very full now, for we've had heavy rains the last week or two. Wouldn't it be exciting to crawl through that hole, when the water was less, and see where it led to!"

"Where does the River Spelter rise?" asked Tom. "In this same mountain?"

"Nobody knows," said Sandy. Tom looked astonished.

"But hasn't anyone followed it up to see?" he asked.

"No," said Sandy with a laugh. "It's like this burn here – it suddenly flows out of the mountain, and no one has ever dared to seek its source, for it would mean swimming against a strong current, in pitch-black darkness, underwater! And who would care to do that?"

"How peculiar," said Tom thoughtfully. "This is a more exciting place than I thought – springs that gush out of rocks, and rivers that come from underground homes – and strange men that live in secret tumbledown huts!"

"Let's start home again now," said Sandy, suddenly remembering the two men and their dog. "It's stopped raining. Tom, remind me to tell you something when we get back."

Down the mountain they went and poor Sheila quickly decided that it was far worse to go down steep slopes than to go up them! She was tired out when at last they reached Kidillin House.

"Oh, Sandy, you shouldn't have taken Tom and Sheila so far," said Miss Mitchell, when she saw Sheila's white, tired face. "And look – the child's soaked through!"

Sandy and Jeanie were ashamed of themselves when they saw that Sheila really was too tired even to eat. They went to tie up Mack, and to let Paddy loose.

"Anyway, we've shown Tom and Sheila what sillies they are when it comes to walking and climbing!" said Sandy. "Oh – where's Tom? I wanted to tell him something!"

He found Tom groaning as he took off his boots. "My poor feet!" he said. "You're a wretch, Sandy – you wait till I find something I can do better than you!"

"Tom," said Sandy. "Listen. I peeped inside the back room of that old tumbledown hut, and do you know, there was a whole lot of machinery there. I don't know what it was – I've never seen anything like it before. Whatever do you think those men keep it there for? Seems funny, doesn't it, in a place like this?"

Tom sat up with a jerk. "Some sort of machinery!" he said in amazement. "What, in that old hut on that desolate mountainside, where there are only a few sheep? How would they get machinery there? There's no road."

"There's a rough road the other side of the mountain," said Sandy. "Easy enough to go over the top, and get down to the path that way – and there's a good road a bit further down the other side, too."

Tom whistled. His eyes grew bright. "I wonder if we've hit on something peculiar!" he said. "We'll tell your father, and see what he says. Perhaps those two men are spies!"

"Don't be silly," said Sandy. "What would spies do here, among the mountains? There's nothing to spy on! Anyway my father is away now."

"All right, Mr Know-All," said Tom. "But we might as well tell your father when he comes back, all the same!"

3

A Chapter of Quarrels

The next day the children began lessons with Miss Mitchell. Tom was most disgusted. "Have I got to learn from a woman?" he said. "I've been used to going to a boys' school. I don't want to learn from a woman."

"Well, Sandy does," said Mrs MacLaren with a laugh. "And he's a pretty hefty boy, isn't he? There is no school here, you see, and until the war is over Sandy must stay at home."

So Tom and Sheila joined Sandy and Jeanie in the schoolroom with Miss Mitchell – and they soon found a way of paying back the two Scottish children for the long walk of the day before! Tom was far ahead of Sandy in arithmetic, and Sheila's writing was beautiful – quite different from Jeanie's scrawl.

"Good gracious! Is that as far as you've got in arithmetic!" said Tom, looking at Sandy's book. "I did those sums years ago! You are a baby!"

Sandy scowled down at his book. He knew he was not good at arithmetic. Miss Mitchell had struggled with him for years.

"Go to your place, Tom," said Miss Mitchell briskly. "Everybody isn't the same. Some are good at one thing and some are good at another. We'll see if your geography is as good as your arithmetic! Perhaps it isn't!"

But it was! Tom was a clever boy, and Sheila was a sharp little girl who read easily and beautifully, and who wrote as well as Miss Mitchell herself.

"I can see that Sheila and I are going to be the top of the class!" said Tom slyly to Sandy, as they went out at eleven o'clock for a break in their lessons. "You may be able to beat us at climbing mountains, Sandy – but we'll beat you at lesson-time! Why, Jeanie writes like a baby!"

"I don't!" said Jeanie, almost in tears.

"Yes, you do," said Sheila. "Why, at home even the first class could write better than you can! And you don't even know your twelve times table yet!"

This was quite true. Jeanie did not like lessons, and she had never troubled to try really hard to learn all her tables. Poor Miss Mitchell had been in despair over her many times.

But Jeanie was not going to have her English cousins laughing at her. She made up her mind to learn all her tables perfectly as soon as she could. This was hard for her, because Jeanie would not usually spend any of her playtime doing anything but climbing the hills, swimming in the river, and driving round the lanes in the pony-trap or the waggonette.

Secretly Miss Mitchell was pleased that Tom and Sheila were ahead of Jeanie and Sandy. Now perhaps her two pupils would feel ashamed, and would work much harder.

"And it won't do Tom and Sheila any harm to find that they can't do the walking and climbing that our two can," thought Miss Mitchell. "After a few quarrels they will all settle down and be happy together."

The two dogs eyed one another and tried to boast to one another in their own way. Paddy could do plenty of tricks, and whenever he wanted a biscuit he sat up on his hind legs in a comical way. Then Tom would put a biscuit on his nose, and say, "Trust, Paddy, trust!"

Paddy would not eat the biscuit until Tom said "Paid for!" Then he would toss the biscuit into the air, catch it, and gobble it up.

Mack watched this trick scornfully. He wasn't going to do any tricks for his food! Not he! If he wanted anything extra he'd go out and catch a rabbit. He was very proud of the fact that he could run as fast as a rabbit, and had three times brought a rabbit home to Sandy. Could Paddy do that? Mack barked to Paddy and asked him.

Paddy didn't answer. He lay curled up by Tom's feet, his eyes on Mack, ready to fly at him if he came any nearer. Mack whined scornfully, and then got up. He meant to show Paddy what he could do.

"Woof?" he said enquiringly. Paddy got up too. He knew that Mack wanted him to go out with him, and though he was still on his guard, he thought it would be fun to go into the hills with this dog, which knew the way about.

"Look at that!" said Sandy in surprise. "That's the first time that Paddy has gone with Mack without flying at him."

The two dogs trotted out of doors, Paddy a good way behind. He could see the tiniest wag in Mack's tail and so he trusted him – but if that wag stopped, then Paddy was ready to pounce on him!

Out of the corner of his eye Mack saw Paddy's tail too. He could see the tiniest wag there also. Good. As long as that little wag was there, Mack knew that Paddy would not fling himself on him!

So, each watching the other carefully, the dogs went out on the hills. And then Mack began to show off to Paddy. He spied a rabbit under a bush and gave chase. The rabbit tore down a burrow. Mack started up another one and that went down a burrow too. Then Paddy started up a young rabbit, but it was away and up the hill before he had even seen which way it went!

"Woof! *Watch me!*" barked Mack, and he tore after a big rabbit so fast that he snapped at its white bobtail before it could get down a burrow. Mack walked back to Paddy with the bit of white fluff still in his mouth.

Paddy turned his head away, pretending not to look, and then began to scratch himself. He wasn't going to tell this boastful dog that he thought it was jolly clever to catch a rabbit's tail – though secretly he couldn't help admiring Mack very much for his speed and strength. After he had scratched himself well, he got up and trotted back to the house.

"I'm tired of this silly game," his tail seemed to say to Mack. Mack followed him in, disappointed. Paddy waited till Mack was in the room, and then he stood on his hind legs and shut the door! This was another of his tricks, and people always thought it was very clever.

"Goodness! Did you see Paddy shut the door?" said Jeanie, quite astonished. "Mack! You can't do that, old boy! You'd better learn!"

Mack was angry. He growled. What! Here he had just been smart enough to catch a rabbit's tail –

and now this silly dog had shut the door and been praised for a stupid thing like that. Dear me – and Sheila was giving him a biscuit for his cleverness! Well, why didn't Sandy give him a biscuit for his smartness with rabbits?

And so both the dogs and the children were angry with the other's boasting, and would not be friends. Out-of-doors the Scottish cousins were far and away better than the English pair, and could run faster, jump higher and climb further, but indoors Tom and Sheila shone. Their lessons were done more quickly and better than their cousins, and they could learn anything by heart in a few minutes.

"It takes me half an hour to learn this bit of poetry," grumbled Sandy. He was bent over "Horatius keeps the Bridge". He liked the story in it, but it was so difficult to learn.

"How slow you are!" laughed Tom. "It took me just five minutes. I can say it straight off now – listen!"

"Oh, be quiet, you boaster!" growled Sandy, putting his hands over his ears. "I wish you'd never come! You make Miss Mitchell think that Jeanie and I are as stupid as sheep, and she's always scolding us."

There was silence. Tom and Sheila said nothing

at all. Sandy began to feel uncomfortable. He looked up. Tom had gone very red, and Sheila looked as if she was going to cry.

Tom got up and spoke stiffly. "I'm sorry you wish we'd never come. We didn't think we were as bad as all that. But seeing that you have said what you really thought, I'll also say what I think. I wish we had never come too. Sheila and I have done our best to keep up with you in your walking and climbing because we didn't want you to think we were weak and feeble. But we're not used to mountains and it would have been kinder of you if you'd let us go a bit slower at first. However, I suppose that's too much to expect."

"And I'd like to say something too!" burst out Sheila. "You're always boasting about your wonderful mountains and the brown bur-r-rns, and the purple heather-r-r-r — but we would rather have the things we know. We'd like to see the big London buses we love, and our tall policemen, and to see the trains. We'd like to see more people about, and to go in the parks and play with our own friends at the games we know. It's p-p-p-perfectly horrid b-b-being here — and I w-w-w-want my m-m-m-mother!"

She burst into tears. Jeanie was horrified. Had they really been as unkind as all that? She ran over to Sheila and tried to put her arms round her cousin. But Sheila pushed her away fiercely. Tom went over and hugged his sister.

"Cheer up," he said. "When the war's over we'll go back home. Sandy and Jeanie will be glad to be rid of us then – but we'll make the best of it till we go."

Sandy wanted to say a lot of things but he couldn't say a word. He was ashamed of himself. After all, his cousins were his guests. How could he have said to them that he wished they had never come? What would his mother and father say if they knew? Scottish people were famous for the welcome they gave to friends.

Tom thought that Sandy was sulking, and he looked at him in disgust. "I'm sorry Sheila and I are a bit more forward in our lessons than you," he said. "But we can't help that any more than you can help knowing your old mountains better than we do. Sheila, do stop crying. Here comes Aunt Jessie."

Jeanie looked up in alarm. If Mother came in and wanted to know why Sheila was crying and found out – my goodness, there would be trouble! She and Sandy would be sent to bed at once, and have nothing but bread and water!

Sheila stopped crying at once. She bent her head

over her book. Tom went to his place and began to mutter his poetry to himself – so when Mother came into the room she saw four children all working hard, and did not know that two of them were ashamed and frightened, that one was angry and hurt and the fourth one was very miserable and homesick.

She looked round. "What, still doing lessons?" she said.

"It's some poetry Miss Mitchell gave us to learn before we went out," explained Tom. "We've nearly finished."

"Well, finish it this evening," said Mother. "It's half past two now, and a lovely day. Would you all like to take your tea out somewhere on the hills, and have a picnic? You won't be able to do it much longer, when the mists come down."

"Oh yes, Mother, do let's have a picnic!" cried Jeanie, flinging down her book. She always loved a picnic. "We'll go and find some blackberries."

"Very well," said Mother. "Go and get ready and I'll pack up your tea."

She went out. Jeanie spoke to Sheila. "It was nice of you not to let Mother see you were crying," she said. Sheila said nothing. She looked miserably at Jeanie. She did not want to climb mountains for a picnic. But there was no help for it. It was such a hilly country that sooner or later you had to climb, no matter in what direction you went!

The girls went to their room. Jeanie pulled out some comfortable old shoes and took them to Sheila. "Look," she said. "Wear these, Sheila. They are old and strong, much better for climbing than the shoes you wear. Mother is getting some strong shoes for you next time she goes into the town."

They fitted Sheila well. Jeanie gave her an old tammy instead of a straw hat. Then they went downstairs to find the boys.

Sandy still hadn't said a word to Tom. He just couldn't. He always found it very difficult to say he was sorry about anything. But he found a good stick and handed it to Tom, knowing that it would make climbing a good deal easier.

Tom took it – but he put it in a corner of the room when Sandy was not looking! He would dearly have loved to take it, but he wasn't going to have Sandy thinking he needed a stick, like an old man! Jeanie saw him put the stick away and she went to Sandy.

"Sandy!" she whispered. "Tom would like the stick, I know, and so would Sheila – but they won't have them if they think we don't take them too. So let's take one each, and then the others won't mind."

This was rather clever of Jeanie! For as soon as Tom saw that Jeanie and Sandy had also found sticks for themselves he at once went to take his from the corner where he had put it! After all, if his cousins used a stick, there was no reason why he shouldn't as well!

They set off. They allowed both dogs to come, for although they were still not good friends the two dogs put up with one another better now.

Tom and Sandy carried a bag each on their backs, full of the picnic things.

"I say! Let's go up to that funny old hut again, and see if those two men are still there!" said Tom, who always liked an adventure. "I'd like to peep into that back room if I could, and find that machine that Sandy saw."

"But isn't that too far?" said Jeanie, anxious to show that she could consider others. Tom shook his head stoutly. He was beginning to get used to the hills now.

"I can help Sheila over the bad bits," he said, "and now that she's got strong shoes on, and a good stick, she'll be all right, won't you, Sheila?"

"Yes," said Sheila bravely – though her heart sank at the thought of the long climb again.

"All right then," said Sandy. "We'll go up to the hut and see what we can find!"

4

A Walk and a Surprise

They set off. Sheila did not find the climb so hard as she thought. She was getting used to walking in the hilly country now, and besides, Jeanie's shoes were well-made for climbing and were very comfortable. So Sheila walked well and began to enjoy herself.

"We'll have our tea when we get to that clump of birch trees," said Jeanie, when they had climbed for some time. "There's a marvellous view from there. We can see the steamers going by, it's such a clear day!" So, when they reached the birches, they all sat down and undid the picnic bags. There were tomato sandwiches, hard-boiled eggs, with a screw of salt to dip them into, brown bread and butter, buttered scones, and some fine currant cake. The children ate hungrily, and looked far away to where the sea shone blue in the autumn sunshine.

"There goes a steamer!" said Jeanie, pointing to where a grey steamer slid over the water. "And there's another."

"Over there is where the *Yelland* went down," said Sandy, pointing to the east. "And not far from it the *Harding* was torpedoed too. I hope those steamers will be all right that we are watching now."

"Of course they will," said Tom lazily. "I bet there's no submarine round about here!"

Jeanie cleared up the litter and packed the bits of paper back into the bags. Her mother was always very strict about litter, and it had to be brought back and burned, never left lying about.

"Well, what about creeping up to see if we can spot what's in that back room?" said Tom, getting up. "I'm well rested now. What about you, Sheila?"

"Sheila can stay here with me," said Jeanie, quickly. "I don't want to go any further today. We'll wait here till you come back."

Sheila looked at Jeanie gratefully. She was tired, and did not really want to go any further, but she would not have said so for anything!

Sandy looked at Jeanie in amazement and was just going to tease her for being lazy, when his sister winked quickly at him. That wink said as plainly as anything: "Sheila's tired but won't say so – so I'll pretend I am, and then she won't mind staying here."

"All right, Jeanie," said Sandy. "Tom and I will

go and we'll take the two dogs."

So off went the two boys, each with his stick, though Sandy kept forgetting to use his and tucked it under his arm. Tom was glad to have the help of his, though, and it made a great difference to the climb.

When they had almost come in sight of the old cottage, Tom stopped. "I think one of us had better stay here a few minutes with the dogs," he said. "The other can creep through the heather and find out whether the men are about – and that dog they spoke of. I don't want to be a dog's dinner!"

"All right," said Sandy. "Take the dogs, Tom. I'll go. I know the way better than you do."

So Tom held the two dogs, and Sandy wriggled through the heather silently until he came in sight of the old cottage. No one seemed to be about. The door was shut. No dog barked.

Sandy wriggled closer. Not a sound was to be heard. No smoke came from the chimney. Sandy suddenly got up and ran to the old cottage. He peered in at the front window. The place was empty, though the furniture was still there.

It only took the boy a minute or two to make sure that no one, man or dog, was about. He ran to the edge of the heather and whistled to Tom. Up he came with the two dogs.

"There's no one here," said Sandy. "We'll go in and I'll show you that funny machinery with all its knobs and handles and things."

They tried the door. It was locked! Sandy put his hefty shoulder to it and pushed but the lock was good and strong and would not give an inch.

"They've put a new lock on it," said the boy in disappointment. "It never used to have a lock at all. Well, let's go and look in through the back window."

They went round to the back of the cottage. But there they had a surprise!

"They've boarded up the window inside!" said Sandy in amazement. "We can't see a thing! Not a thing! Oh blow! I did want to show you what was in that little room, Tom."

"It's funny," said Tom thoughtfully, rubbing his chin and frowning. "Why should they do that? It means that the machinery, whatever it is, is still in there, and they've boarded it up in case we come back and spy around. I do wish we could get into the house."

But it was no good wishing. The door was locked and bolted, the one front window was fastened tightly, and the back one was boarded up so well that not even a chink was left for peeping through.

"Well, we can't see anything, that's certain," said Tom. "Let's go and have a look at that stream coming out of the hillside through that rock, Sandy. I'd like to see that again."

The boys went there. The water still poured out of the curious hole but there was not so much of it as before.

"That's because we haven't had so much rain this week," explained Sandy. Tom nodded. He went to the hole and peered into it. "If the water goes down much more we could easily get in there," he said. "I'd love to see where that water comes from. I read a book written by a Frenchman, Sandy, who explored heaps of underground streams and caves in France, and crawled through holes like that."

"What did he find?" asked Sandy, interested.

"He found wonderful caves and underground halls and pits, and he found where some mysterious rivers had their beginnings," said Tom. "I'll show you the book when we get home. You know, if only we could get past that spring pouring out from the rock, we might find extraordinary caverns where no foot had ever trodden before!"

Tom was getting excited. His eyes shone, and he made Sandy feel excited too. "Might there be a cave or something in this mountain then?" he asked.

"There might be heaps," said Tom. "And maybe somewhere in this great mountain is the beginning of the River Spelter. You told me that it comes out from underground and that no one knows where it rises."

Sandy's eyes shone now. This was the most exciting thing he had ever heard of. "Tom, we must explore this," he said. "We must! If only those men weren't here – they will send us away if they see us. I wish I knew what they were up to."

"So do I," said Tom. "When your father comes back, we'll tell him about them, Sandy, and about the odd machinery they've hidden in that back room."

A rabbit suddenly appeared on the hillside and looked cheekily at the two dogs, who were sitting quietly by the boys. At once both Paddy and Mack barked loudly and tore at the rabbit.

It did a strange thing. It shot up the hillside, leaped over the boys, and then disappeared into a burrow just beside the spring that gushed from the rock. And then Paddy did an even stranger thing!

He shot after the rabbit but was stopped by the water. He leaped right over the water, saw the hole in the rock through which the spring flowed – and shot into the hole! He thought the rabbit had gone there!

He didn't come out. He disappeared completely. The two boys gaped at one another, and then Tom called his dog sharply.

"Paddy! Paddy! Come here!"

No Paddy came. Only a frightened whining could be heard from inside the hole. Paddy must have got right through the water and be sitting somewhere beyond.

"Paddy! Come out!" cried Tom anxiously. "You got in so you can get out! Come on now!"

But Paddy was terrified. The noise of the water inside the rock was tremendous, and the dog was terribly afraid. He had managed to scramble to a rocky shelf above the flow of the spring, and was sitting there, trembling. He could hardly hear the shouts of his master because of the noise the water made.

"Now what are we to do?" said Tom, in dismay. "He's right inside that rock. Paddy! PADDY, you idiot!"

But Paddy did not appear. Sandy looked worried. They must get the dog somehow.

Tom looked at Sandy. "Well, I suppose he'll come out sometime," he said. "Had we better wait any longer? The girls will be getting worried."

"We can't leave your dog," said Sandy. He knew that Tom loved Paddy as much as he loved Mack. Mack was looking astonished. He could not imagine where Paddy had gone!

Sandy climbed up to the rock, and looked into the hole. The rushing water wetted him, and spray flew into his face.

"I believe I could wriggle through the water today," he said. "It's not very deep and not very strong. I could find old Paddy and push him out for you."

"Oh no, Sandy," said Tom. "You'd get soaked, and you might hurt yourself. You don't know what's behind that spring!"

Sandy was stripping off his clothes. He grinned at Tom. "I don't mind if I do get soaked now," he said. "I'll just hang myself out to dry, if I do!"

5

A Rescue and a Strange Discovery

Sandy climbed right up to the hole again, and then began to push himself into it. It was more than big enough for his body. As he wriggled, the cold water soaked him, and sometimes his face was under the surface, so that he had to hold his breath. His body blocked up the light that came in from the hole, and everything looked black as night. It was very strange.

He felt about as he went through the hole. It widened almost at once, behind the opening, and became higher and more spacious. The water became shallower too. Sandy sat up in the water, and felt about with his hand. He felt the rocky ceiling a little above him, and on one side was a rocky shelf. His hand touched wet hair!

"Paddy!" he cried. "You poor thing! Go on out of the hole, you silly!" His voice was almost drowned in the sound of the rushing water around him, but Paddy heard it and was comforted. He jumped down into the water beside Sandy. Sandy pushed him towards the hole.

Paddy was taken by the swirl of the water and lost his balance. The water took him like a floating log and he was rushed to the opening, struggling with all his feet. He shot out with the spring, and fell at Tom's feet.

Tom was delighted. He picked up the wet dog and hugged him, and then Paddy struggled down to shake the water from his hair. Mack came up and sniffed him in astonishment.

"Been swimming?" he seemed to say. "What an extraordinary idea!"

Sandy was still in the rocky hole. He was getting used to the darkness now. He sat up on the shelf where he had found Paddy, and felt about with his hands. Then he made his way a little further up the stream. The rocky ceiling got quickly higher – and then Sandy found himself in a great cave, at the bottom of which the stream rushed along with a noise that echoed all around.

It was so dark that Sandy could hardly see the shape of the cave. He only sensed that it rose high and was wide and spacious. He was filled with astonishment and excitement, and went back to tell Tom.

But meanwhile something was happening outside! Tom had heard voices and, peeping round the bend, he had seen in the distance the two men returning to their cottage! With them was a large dog.

Tom called in through the hole. "Sandy! Sandy! Quick! Come back!"

Sandy was already coming back. He sat down in the water when the ceiling fell low, and then, as it became lower still, the boy had to lie full length in the water, and wriggle along like that, the stream sometimes going right over his face. He got to the opening at last, and Tom helped him down.

"Sandy! Hurry! The men are back!" whispered Tom. "They've got a dog too, and he may hear us at any moment. Put on your things quickly."

Sandy tried to be quick. But his body was cold from the icy water, and he could not make his hands pull on his things quickly over his wet body. He shook and shivered with the cold, and Tom did his best to help him to dress.

He was just putting on his jacket when the men's dog came sniffing round the corner! When he saw the boys and the dogs he stood still, and the fur on his neck rose high with rage! He barked loudly.

"Quick!" said Tom to Sandy. "We must go. Let's go down this way and maybe the men won't see us!"

So the two boys hurried round a bend, where

bracken grew tall, and began to make their way through it. The dog still barked loudly, and the two men came running to him.

"What is it? Who is it?" cried one of them. "Go on, find him, find him!"

The fat man shouted something too, but the boys could not understand what he said. They were creeping down the hillside, glad that the men had not yet seen them. But the dog heard them, and came bounding after them.

"Now we're done for!" groaned Tom, as he saw the big dog leaping down towards them. He grasped his stick firmly. But someone else stood

before him! It was Paddy, his wet fur bristling and his throat almost bursting with fierce growls. Mack joined him, his teeth bared. Side by side the two dogs glared at the enemy, who when he saw two of them, stopped still and considered. He was bigger than either – but they were two!

The men were following their dog. "Come on, Tom," whispered Sandy. "Let the dogs settle it for us. We must get back to the girls quickly."

They wriggled through the bracken and heather, slid down a stony piece unseen, and then made their way to where the girls were waiting anxiously. The boys had been a very long time.

"Sh!" said Sandy, as Jeanie opened her mouth to shout a welcome. And just as he said that a tremendous noise broke out – a noise of barking and howling and whining and yelping and growling and snarling!

"Good gracious!" said Jeanie, starting up. "Are the dogs fighting?"

"Yes – fighting a big dog together!" said Sandy. "Come on, we must go while the dogs are keeping off the men. They haven't seen us yet and we don't want them to."

"But will the dogs be all right?" panted Sheila as they ran down the hillside.

"Of course!" said Sandy. "Our Mack is more

than a match for two other dogs, and I reckon your Paddy is too!"

The children stopped when they reached a big gorse bush and sat down behind it, panting. They were safe there, for an old shepherd's shelter was nearby, and Loorie, the shepherd, was pottering about in the distance. In a few hurried words the boys told the girls all that had happened.

Tom stared when Sandy told of the cave behind the rock where the spring gushed out. "I was right then!" he cried. "I say, what fun! We must go and explore that when we get a chance. If only those men weren't there."

"Perhaps they won't be there long, once my father hears about them," said Sandy grimly. "I think they are spies of some sort. I guess the police would like to see what is in their back room too!"

"I wish those dogs would come back," said Sheila, looking worried, for she hated to think that Paddy might be bitten by the big dog.

No sooner had she spoken than the two dogs appeared, looking extremely pleased with themselves! Paddy's right ear was bleeding, and Mack's left ear looked the worse for wear — but otherwise they seemed quite all right.

They trotted up to the children together and sat down, looking proud and pleased. Mack licked

Paddy's ear. Paddy sniffed in a friendly way at Mack and then, putting out a paw, pawed him as if he wanted a game.

"Why, they're good friends now!" cried Jeanie in surprise. "They like each other!"

Tom and Sandy looked at one another. Jeanie looked at Sheila.

"It's time we were friends too," said Tom, with a red face. "Thanks, Sandy, for rescuing Paddy from that hole. It was jolly good of you – getting into that icy-cold water and wriggling up a narrow rocky hole. You're a good sort."

"So are you," said Sandy. "I'm sorry for what I said. I didn't mean it. I was only mad because you were better at arithmetic than I was. I'm glad you came, really."

"Shake!" said Tom, with a laugh, and he held out his hand to Sandy. "We're friends now, and we'll stick by each other, won't we – just like the two dogs!"

The girls stared at the boys, glad to see that they were friends now. Jeanie held out her hand to Sheila. She would have liked to hug her, but she thought it looked grander to shake hands like the boys. Sheila solemnly shook her hand, and then they all began to laugh.

6

A Disappointment – and a Picnic

Things began to happen very quickly after that exciting day. For one thing Captain MacLaren, Sandy's father, returned home on forty-eight hours' leave, and the children and Mrs MacLaren told him about the mysterious men in the old cottage on the mountain.

Captain MacLaren was astonished and puzzled. He was inclined to think that Sandy was making too much of the curious "machinery" he had seen in the back room. However, when he heard that one man had called the other "Carl", he decided that he had better tell the police.

"Carl is a German name," he said. "I can't imagine why German spies could possibly want to hide themselves away on such a lonely hillside, but you never know! They may be up to something odd. I'll ring up the police."

He did so – and two solemn Scots policemen came riding out to Kidillin House on their bicycles, with notebooks and pencils to take down anything the children were able to tell them.

"We'll go up to the cottage and investigate, Captain," said the sergeant, shutting his notebook with a snap. "It's a wee bit unlikely we'll be finding anything to make a noise about, but we'll go."

They knew where the cottage was, and they set off to find it that afternoon. The children were very excited. Miss Mitchell could hardly get them to do any sums, French, or history at all. Even her star pupil, Tom, made all kinds of silly mistakes, and when he confused the number of shillings in a pound with the number of pennies, the governess put down her pencil in despair.

"This won't do," she said. "You are not thinking of what you are doing. What *are* you thinking of?"

But the four children wouldn't tell her! They were thinking of the exciting cave that Sandy had discovered behind the stream! They hadn't said a word about this to the grown-ups, because they were afraid that if they did they might be forbidden to explore it – and how could they bear to promise such a thing?

"We'll tell Mother as soon as we know exactly what's behind that hole," said Sandy. "We'll take our torches, and we'll explore properly. We might find strange cave pictures done by men hundreds of years ago! We might find old stone arrowheads and all kinds of exciting things!"

Sandy had been reading Tom's book. This book told of the true adventures of a Frenchman who had been exploring underground caves and rivers, and of all the wonderful pictures he had found drawn on the walls and ceilings of the hidden caves. Sandy was simply longing to do some exploring himself now.

Miss Mitchell decided that it was no use doing any more lessons until the policemen came back from the old cottage. She was feeling a bit excited herself, and guessed what the children's feelings must be like. So she told them to shut their books, and go to do some gardening. Sandy and Jeanie each had their own gardens, and Tom and Sheila had been given a patch too.

"It is time to dig up your old beans and to cut down your summer plants, Sandy," said Miss Mitchell. "Tom, you can help the gardener to sweep up the leaves. Sheila, you can help Jeanie to get down the beanpoles."

The children ran off, shouting in joy. From the garden they would be able to see the policemen when they came down from the mountain.

"They'll have the two spies with them!" said Sandy.

"Yes, and maybe they'll be handcuffed together," said Tom, sweeping up the leaves as if they were spies! "I wonder if they'll make the dog a prisoner too!"

"I guess our two dogs gave him a rough time!" said Jeanie. She looked at Mack and Paddy, who were tearing round and round after each other. Jeanie had doctored their ears well, and they were healing quickly. She was very good with animals. "They're jolly good friends now!" said Jeanie, pleased. "I'm glad we don't have to tie up first one and then another."

"I wonder how the police will get that machinery down the mountain," said Tom, stopping his sweeping for a moment.

"Same way as it was got up, I expect!" said Sandy. "On somebody's back! I expect it was taken up in pieces from the road the other side of the mountain."

"Look!" said Sheila suddenly. "Here come the policemen! Auntie! Uncle! Miss Mitchell! Here come the policemen."

In great excitement the children ran to the gate. But to their disappointment they saw that the two policemen coming down the hillside were alone. The men were not with them!

"I wonder why," said Tom.

"Perhaps they weren't there," suggested Jeanie. The policemen came up to Kidillin House and

smiled as the children rained questions on them.
Only when Captain MacLaren came out to see
them did they say what had happened.

"Yes, sir, there are two men there all right," said
the sergeant. "They say that they left London
because of their fear of air-raids, and took that little
cottage for safety. I asked them to let me look all
over it – and there's no machinery of any sort
there. I think yon boy of yours must have imagined
it. There's no place round the old cottage where
they could hide anything either."

"I didn't imagine it!" cried Sandy. "I didn't!"

"Did any of the others see it?" asked the
sergeant, looking at Tom, Sheila, and Jeanie.

"No," they said. "But we saw the windows
boarded up!"

"They say they did that for the black-out," said
the second policeman. "They've curtains for the
front room but none for the back."

"Pooh! As if they'd bother to black out windows
that look right on to the mountain behind!" said
Tom, scornfully. "All a made-up tale!"

"One man is deaf and dumb," said the sergeant.
"We got all the talk from the dark man."

That made the children stare even more. Both
Tom and Sandy had heard the two men talking.
Why then did one pretend to be deaf and dumb?

The policemen jumped on to their bicycles and rode off, saluting the captain. The children gathered together in a corner of the garden and began to talk.

"What have they done with the machinery?"

"Why did one pretend to be dumb?"

"What a stupid reason for boarding up the window!"

"I guess I know why one pretended to be dumb! I bet he talks English with a German accent! I bet if he answered the policeman's questions, he would give himself away at once!" This was Tom speaking, and the others listened to him.

"Yes, that's it!" went on the excited boy. "He's the one called Carl – he's a German all right. It's an old trick to pretend to be dumb if you don't want to give yourself away!"

"And they guessed we might tell the police so they hid their machinery quickly," said Sandy. "But didn't have time to unboard the windows."

"That's it," said Tom. There was a silence while they all thought quickly. Then, "Hey! I think I know!" he cried, in such an excited voice that they all jumped. "They've taken it to pieces, and managed somehow to get it into the cave behind the stream! That's what they've done. Somehow or other they must have known about that cave."

"It would be easy enough to do that, if the two of them worked together," said Sandy, thinking hard. "They could wrap the pieces in oiled cloth, tie them to ropes – and then one man could climb back to the cave and pull up the rope whenever the other man tied the packets on to it. It is sure to be able to break down into pieces, that machine – how else could they have got it up to the cottage so secretly?"

"We've hit on their secret all right," said Tom, and his face glowed. "Now what we've got to do is quite simple."

"What's that?" asked all the others.

"Why, all we've got to do is to go up to the cottage, lie low till the men go shopping or something, and then explore that cave again," said Tom. "If we find the machinery is there, we'll know we're right, and we can slip down to the police at once!"

"Oh good!" said Sandy. "The girls could keep watch for us, Tom, and you and I could take our bathing-suits and wriggle through the hole."

"Is there time today?" wondered Tom, looking at his watch. But there wasn't. It was a nuisance, because all the children were longing to go on with their big adventure and now they would have to wait until the next day!

Fortunately for them the next day was Saturday. They begged their governess to let them take their lunch on the hills. Mrs MacLaren had gone to the town to see her husband off once more, and Miss Mitchell was in charge.

"Very well," said Miss Mitchell. "I think I'll come with you today. I've nothing much to do."

The children stared at one another in dismay. If Miss Mitchell came they couldn't do anything! They could not think of a single reason to give her to stop her coming.

"I'll go and ask Cook to get a good lunch ready," said Miss Mitchell, bustling out to the kitchen. "I'll pack it up nicely in the picnic bags."

"Well, isn't that awful!" said Sheila, as the governess went out of the room. "What can we do to stop her coming?"

They thought and thought – but it was no good. She would have to come!

"Well, listen," said Tom at last. "After we have had our picnic, you two girls can stay with Miss Mitchell, and Sandy and I will slip off to explore again. That's the only thing we can do."

"But we wanted to come too!" wailed Sheila.

"Well, you can't!" said Tom. "Now for goodness sake don't make a fuss, Sheila, or Miss Mitchell will begin to think something's up!"

But Miss Mitchell didn't guess anything at all. She packed up the lunch, gave it to the two boys to carry on their backs, and soon they were all ready to start.

"Got your torch, Sandy?" whispered Tom.

"Yes," whispered back Sandy. "And I've got my bathing-suit on under my clothes too!"

They all set off. They climbed up the sunny hillside, chattering and laughing, picking blackberries as they went. Miss Mitchell was glad to see them all such good friends now, even the two dogs! They chased rabbits, real and imaginary, all the time, and once Paddy got so far down a hole that he had to be pulled out by Tom.

The boys made their way towards the cottage. Miss Mitchell was not sure she wanted to go there.

"Those men won't like us spying around," she said. "They probably guess that it is you children who had the police sent up there."

"Well, we'll not go too near," said Sandy. "What about having our lunch here, Miss Mitchell? There's a beautiful view for you to look at."

Miss Mitchell knew the view well. It was the same one that the children had looked at before when they watched the steamers going by, far away on the blue sea. They all sat down, glad of a rest.

"There's a steamer," said Tom.

"Yes," said Miss Mitchell, looking at it through the pair of binoculars she had brought. "I hope it won't be sunk. Those coastal steamers should go in convoys, but they won't be bothered — and two were sunk the other day."

"What were they?" asked Sandy. "The *Yelland* and the *Harding*, do you mean?"

"No, two others have been sunk since then," said Miss Mitchell. "By a submarine too — so there must be one lurking about somewhere."

The children looked at the little steamer slipping slowly along, and hoped that it would not be sunk. Miss Mitchell opened the picnic bags and handed out ham sandwiches, tomatoes, hard-boiled eggs, apples, jam-tarts and ginger buns.

"Ooooh! What a gorgeous picnic!" said Sheila, who was rapidly getting as big an appetite as her Scottish cousins. There was creamy milk to drink too. The dogs had one large biscuit each and little bits of ham that the children pulled from their sandwiches. Everybody was very happy.

"Goodness me, the sun's hot!" said Miss Mitchell, after they had all eaten as much as they could. "You had better have a little rest before we go on — we really can't climb higher, on top of our enormous lunch!"

She lay back on the warm heather and put her

hat over her eyes. The children sat as still as mice. The same thought came into everyone's head. Would Miss Mitchell go to sleep?

For five minutes nobody said a single word. Even the dogs lay quiet. Then Jeanie gave a little cough. Miss Mitchell didn't stir. Jeanie spoke in a low voice. "Miss Mitchell!"

No answer from Miss Mitchell. Jeanie leaned over her governess, and lifted Miss Mitchell's hat up gently so that she could see if the governess was really asleep.

Her eyes were fast shut and she was breathing deeply. Jeanie nodded to the others. Very quietly they got up from the heather, shaking their fingers at the two dogs to warn them to be quiet. They climbed up higher, rounded a bend in the hillside, and then began to giggle.

"Good!" said Tom, at last. "We've got away nicely. Now come on quickly, everyone. We haven't a minute to lose!"

They climbed quickly towards the old cottage, keeping a good look-out as they went. Would the two men be about? Would they be able to do any exploring? They all felt tremendously excited, and their hearts beat loudly and fast.

7

Miss Mitchell Is Very Cross

Slowly and quietly the children crept over the heather that surrounded the cottage. Mack and Paddy crept with them, joining in what they thought was some new game.

No one was about. The dog was not to be seen either. "I'll just creep over to the cottage and see what I can see!" whispered Sandy. So off he went, running quietly to the hut. He peeped cautiously in at a window – and then drew back very quickly indeed.

He came back to the others. "The two men are there," he whispered. "But they are sound asleep, like Miss Mitchell! This must be a sleepy afternoon! Come on – we'll go to the underground burn, and see if we can get into the cave and look round before the men wake up."

In great delight the four children crept quietly off to where the big rock jutted out, through which the water fell down the mountainside. But when they came in sight of it, what a shock they got! Tied up beside the rock was the big dog!

The children stopped in dismay. Tom pushed them back, afraid that the dog would see or hear them. They stared at one another, half frightened.

"It's no good trying any exploring this afternoon!" said Tom, frowning in disappointment. "Absolutely no good at all. But it shows one thing plainly – they're afraid we may guess their hiding-place and explore it – so they've put the dog there to guard it!"

"Well, we can't possibly get past that big brute," said Sandy. "I wonder now if there are any signs of trampling round about the burn there, Tom. If they've hidden anything in that cave, they'd have to stand around the rock a good bit, and the footmarks would show. I've a good mind to creep nearer and see."

"No, let me," said Tom at once. He always liked to be the one to do things if he could – and Sandy had done the exploring last time! Tom felt it was his turn.

"Tom! Come back!" whispered Sandy, as Tom crept forward on hands and knees. "I can go much more quietly than you!"

But Tom would not turn back. It was a pity he didn't for suddenly he knelt on a dry twig which cracked in two like a pistol shot!

The dog, lying quietly by the rock, raised up its

head at once and then leaped to its feet, sniffing the air. Tom crouched flat — but the dog saw him. It began to bark loudly, and the mountainside rang and echoed with its loud voice.

"Quick! Get down the slope, back to Miss Mitchell!" said Sandy. "Those men will be out in a minute!"

Sandy was right. The two men woke up at once when they heard the barking of the dog. The door of the cottage opened and out they ran. One of them shouted loudly, "What is it, Digger, what is it?"

Then he saw the children disappearing down the hillside and with a cry of rage he followed them. "Loose the dog!" he yelled to the other man. The children tore away as fast as they could, slipping and sliding as they went.

The dog was loosed — but as soon as he was faced once more by the two dogs who had beaten him the other day he dropped his tail and refused to go after the children. The man shouted at him, but it was no use. Digger was afraid of Mack and Paddy.

But the first man was not afraid of anything! He plunged down the hillside after the children, and just as they reached the place where they had left Miss Mitchell, he caught them up.

Miss Mitchell awoke in a hurry when she heard such a noise of scrambling and shouting. She sat up and looked round. The children ran up to her and the man came up in a rage.

"What are these children doing here?" he shouted. "I tell you, I'll whip them all if they come spying round here. Can't a man be left in peace?"

"I don't know what you are talking about," said Miss Mitchell firmly. "We came up on the hills for a picnic, and we have as much right here as you have. Please go away at once, or I will report you to the police."

The man glared at Miss Mitchell. He began to shout again, but when Miss Mitchell repeated that she would certainly tell the police of his threats to her children, he muttered something and went back up the hillside.

Miss Mitchell was very angry with them. "So you slipped off up to the cottage when I was having a little nap, did you?" she scolded. "Now you see what has happened! You have made enough trouble for those two men already by telling made-up tales about them – and now you go prowling round their cottage again! You will promise me not to go there again."

The children looked at one another in dismay. Just what they hoped wouldn't happen!

"Very well," said Sandy sulkily. "I promise not to go to the cottage again."

"So do I," said Tom. The girls promised too. Miss Mitchell gathered up the picnic things, and said that they must all return home. She really was very cross.

"Miss Mitchell, those weren't made-up tales," said Sandy, as they went down the mountainside. "You shouldn't say that. You know we tell the truth."

"I don't want to hear any more about it," said the governess. "It is most unpleasant to have a man roaring and shouting at us like that, because of your stupid behaviour. You know quite well that I would not have allowed you to go to the cottage if you had asked me."

Miss Mitchell was cross all that day. But the next day was better, and the children went to church glad that Miss Mitchell seemed to have forgotten about the day before. She had not told their mother about them, so that was good.

When they came out of church there was half an hour before lunch. In the distance the children saw Loorie, the old shepherd. Sandy was fond of him, and asked Miss Mitchell if they might go and talk to him.

Loorie was treating a sheep that had a bad leg.

He nodded to the children, and smiled at Tom and Sheila when Sandy explained that they were his cousins.

"This is an easy time of year for you, isn't it, Loorie?" asked Sandy.

"Oh aye," said the old man, rubbing the sheep's leg with some horrid-smelling black ointment. "The winter's the busy time, when the lambing's on."

He went on to tell Tom and Sheila of all the happenings of the year. The two town children listened in great interest. They could hardly understand the Scottish words the old man used, but they loved to hear them.

"Did you lose any lambs this year, Loorie?" asked Sandy.

"Aye, laddie, I lost too many," said Loorie. "And do you ken where I lost them? Down the old pothole on the mountain up there!"

"What old pothole?" asked Tom, puzzled.

"Oh, it's a peculiar place," explained Sandy. "There's a big hole up there, that goes down for ever so far. The sheep sometimes fall into it and they can never be got out."

"It's funny to sit by the hole," said Jeanie. "You can hear a rushing sound always coming up it."

"Folks do say that's the River Spelter," said

Loorie, setting the sheep on its legs again. "Aye, folks say a mighty lot of things."

"The Spelter!" said Tom, surprised. "Why, do you mean that the Spelter goes under the pothole you're talking about?"

"Maybe it does and maybe it doesn't," said the old shepherd, closing his tin of ointment. "There's funny things in the mountains. Don't you go taking the lassies near that pothole, now, Master Sandy!"

"There's Miss Mitchell calling," said Sandy hurriedly, for he saw by Tom's face that his cousin was longing to go to visit the pothole! "Goodbye, Loorie. We'll see you again soon."

As they ran back to Miss Mitchell, Tom panted out some questions. "Where's the pothole? Is it anywhere near the underground stream? Do you suppose that's the Spelter that runs beneath the pothole, or our stream?"

Sandy didn't know at all. But he knew quite well that before that day was out, Tom would want to go and explore the pothole! Sandy wanted to as well.

"I can't think why I didn't remember the pothole before," thought the boy. "I suppose it was because I've known about it all my life and never thought anything about it."

8

Down the Pothole

That afternoon the four children and the dogs set off to the pothole. They had talked about it excitedly, and Tom felt sure that if there was water at the bottom, it might be the very same stream that poured out of the hole in the rock. If it was, they could get down the hole and follow it up – and maybe come to the cave from behind.

"And then we can see if the spies have hidden their things there!" cried Sandy. "We didn't think there could be another way in – but there may be! What a good thing we had that talk to old Loorie this morning."

They took a good many things with them that afternoon. Both boys had strong ropes tied round their waists. All of them had torches, and Tom had matches and a candle too.

"You see," he explained, "if the air is bad, we can tell it by lighting a candle. If the candle flickers a lot and goes out, we shall know the air is too bad for us. Then we shall have to go back."

They also had towels with them, because Tom

thought they might have to undress and wade through water. They could leave their towels by the pothole and dry themselves when they came back. They all felt excited and important. They were out to catch spies, and to find out their secrets!

Sandy took them round the mountain, in the opposite direction to the one they usually went, and at last brought them to the pothole.

It certainly was a very odd place. It looked like a wide pit, overgrown with heather and brambles – but Sandy explained that when they climbed down into this pit-like dell, they would come to the real pothole, a much narrower pit at one side of the dell.

They climbed down into the dell and Sandy took them to one side. He kicked away some branches, and there below them was the pothole!

"Loorie must have put those branches across to stop the sheep from falling in," said Sandy. "Now just sit beside this hole and listen."

The four of them sat beside the strange hole. It was not very big, not more than a metre wide, and curious bits of blue slate stuck out all around it. The children peered down into the hole, but it was like looking down into an endless well. They could see nothing but blackness.

But they could hear a most mysterious noise

coming up to them! It was like the sound of the wind in the trees, but louder and stranger.

"Yes – that's water rushing along all right," said Tom, sitting up again, his face red with excitement. "But it sounds to me a bigger noise than our little stream could make. It sounds more like the River Spelter rushing along in the heart of the mountain, down to where it flows out at the foot, in the village of Kidillin!"

"Could we possibly get down there?" asked Sandy doubtfully. "Would our ropes be long enough? We don't want any accidents! I don't know how we'd be rescued!"

Tom flashed his torch down the hole. "Look!" he said. "Do you see down there, Sandy, there's a sort of rocky shelf. Well, we may find that all the way down there are these rocky bits to help us. If we have a rope firmly round our waists so that we can't fall, we'll be all right. I'll go down first."

"No, you won't," said Sandy. "I'm better used to climbing. Don't forget that it was you who cracked that twig yesterday and gave warning to the dog. If it had been I who was creeping along, the dog would never have known."

Tom looked angry, then the frown went from his face and he nodded. "All right," he said. "Perhaps it would be best if you went. You're good at this sort of thing and I've never done it before."

"The girls are not to come," said Sandy. "Not today, at any rate. It looks more dangerous than I thought, and anyway, we'll want someone to look after the ropes for us. We will tie the ends to a tree, and the girls can watch that they don't slip."

Neither of the girls made any objection to being left at the top. Both of them thought the pothole looked horrid! They were quite content to let the boys try it first!

They all felt really excited. Sandy tied the ends of their two strong ropes to the trunk of a stout pine tree. He and Tom knotted the other ends round their waists as firmly as they could. Now, even if they fell, their ropes would hold them, and the girls could pull them up in safety!

Sandy went down the pothole first. He let himself slip down to the rocky ledge some way down. His feet caught on it with a jerk. His hands felt about for something to hold.

"Are you all right, Sandy?" asked Tom, flashing his torch down the hole.

"Yes," said Sandy. "I'm feeling to see if there's somewhere to put my feet further down." Sandy was as good as a cat at climbing. He soon found a small ledge for his right foot, and then another for his left.

Bits of slate, stone and soil broke away as he slowly climbed downwards, and fell far below him. The pothole did not go straight down, but curved a little now and again, so that it was not so difficult as Sandy had expected to climb down.

"Come on, Tom!" he called. "If you're careful where to put your feet, it's not too difficult."

Tom began his climb down too. He found it far more difficult than Sandy, for he was not so used to climbing. His feet slithered and slipped, and he cut his hands when he clutched at stones and earth.

The girls at the top were holding on to the boys' ropes, letting them out gradually. Tom's rope jerked and pulled, but Sandy's rope went down smoothly.

As Sandy went down further and further, the noise of rushing water became louder and louder until he could not even hear his own voice when he called to Tom. Tom was kicking out so many stones and bits of earth that they fell round poor Sandy like a hailstorm!

"Stop kicking at the sides of the hole!" yelled Sandy. But Tom couldn't help it. Sandy wished he had put on a hat, to stop the pebbles from hitting his head – but soon, at a bend in the hole, he became free of the "hailstorm", and went downwards comfortably.

It was the first part that was so steep and difficult. It was easier further down, for rocky ledges stuck out everywhere, making it almost like climbing down a ladder.

The noise of the water was deafening. Sandy thought it was so near that he might step into it at any moment. So he switched on his torch and looked downwards. The black water gleamed up at him, topped with white spray where it flowed over out-jutting rocks. It was further down than he had thought.

As he climbed down to the water, the hole widened tremendously and became a cave. Sandy jumped down beside the shouting river, and stood there, half frightened, half delighted.

It was a strange sight, that underground river! It flowed along between rocky walls, black, strong and noisy. It entered the cave by a low tunnel, which was filled to the roof with the water. The river flowed in a rocky bed and entered another black tunnel just near Sandy – but it did not fill this tunnel to the roof. Sandy flashed his torch into the tunnel, and saw that for some way, at any rate, the roof was fairly high, about up to his head.

There was a rattle of stones about him, and Tom came sliding down the walls of the pothole at great speed! He had missed his footing and fallen! But

he had not far to fall and, fortunately for him, his
rope was only just long enough to take him beside
Sandy, and it pulled him up with a jerk before he
fell into the water.

"Good gracious!" said Sandy. "You are in a
hurry!"

"Phew!" said Tom, loosening the rope a little
round his waist. "That wasn't very pleasant. I'm

glad I was fairly near the bottom. My word, the rope did give my waist an awful pull! I say, Sandy! What a marvellous sight this is!"

"The underground world!" said Sandy, flashing his torch around. "Look at that black rushing river, Tom! We've got to wade down that, through that tunnel – see?"

"Oooh!" said Tom. "Where do you suppose it goes to?"

"That's what we've got to find out," said Sandy. "I think myself that away up that other tunnel there, is the source of the Spelter. It probably begins in a collection of springs all running to the same rocky bed in the mountain, and then rushing down together as a river. But really it's not more than a fast stream here, though it makes enough noise for a river!"

"That's because it's underground, and the echoes are peculiar," said Tom. "Also, it's going downhill at a good rate, not flowing gently in an even bed. How deep do you suppose it is, Sandy?"

"We'll have to find out!" said Sandy, beginning to undress. "Hurry up! Got your torch with you? Well, bring it, and bring the oilskin bag too, in case we have to swim and need something waterproof to put our torches in. I've got the candles and matches."

9

In the Heart of the Mountain

Both boys stood in their swimsuits. They shivered, for the air was cold. Sandy put one leg into the rushing stream. The water was icy!

"Oooh!" said Sandy, drawing back his leg quickly! "It's mighty cold, Tom. Just hang on to me a minute, will you, so that I can feel how deep the water is."

Tom held on to his arms. Sandy slipped a foot into the water again. He went in over his knee, and right up to his waist! Then he felt a solid rocky bottom, and stood up, grinning.

"It's all right!" he said. "Only up to my waist, Tom. Come on in and we'll explore the tunnel."

Tom got into the water, and then the two boys began to wade along the noisy stream. It went gradually downwards, and once there was quite a steep drop, making a small waterfall. The boys had to help one another down. It was very cold, for the water was really icy. They were both shivering, and yet felt hot with excitement.

The roof of the tunnel kept about head or

shoulder-high. Once the tunnel widened out again into a small cave, and the boys climbed out of the water and did some violent exercises to warm themselves.

They got back into the water again. It suddenly got narrow and deeper. Deeper and deeper it got until the two boys had to swim. And then, oh dear, the tunnel roof dipped down and almost reached the surface of the water!

"Now what are we to do?" said Tom, in dismay.

"Put your torch into its oilskin bag, to begin with," said Sandy, putting his into the bag, next to the candle and box of matches. "Then it won't get wet. If you'll just wait here for me, Tom, I'll swim underwater a little way and see if the roof rises further on."

"Well, for goodness sake be careful," said Tom, in alarm. "I hope you've got enough breath to swim under the water and back, if the roof doesn't rise! The water may flow for a long way touching the roof."

"If it does, we can go no further," said Sandy. "Don't worry about me! I can swim under water for at least a minute!"

He took a deep breath, plunged under the water, and swam hard. He bobbed his head up, but found that the rocky ceiling still touched the stream. He

went on a little way, and then, when he was nearly
bursting for breath, he found that the roof lifted,
and he could stand with his head out of the water.

He took another deep breath and went back for
Tom. "It's all right," he gasped, coming up beside

him. "You need to take a jolly good breath though. Take one now and come along quickly."

Tom began to splutter under the water before he could stick his head up into the air once more and breathe. Sandy couldn't help laughing at him, and Tom was very indignant.

"Just stop laughing!" he said to Sandy. "I was nearly drowned!"

"Oh no you weren't," said Sandy. "I could easily have pulled you through, Tom. Come on – the next bit is easy. We can swim or wade. Let's swim and get warm."

So they swam along in the deep, black water for some way – and then the tunnel widened out into a great underground hall. It was an odd place. Strange stones gleamed in the light of their torches. Phosphorescent streaks shone in the rocky walls, and here and there curious things hung down from the ceiling rather like icicles.

"Ooh, isn't it odd?" whispered Tom and at once his whisper came back to him in strange echoes. "Isn't it odd, isn't it odd – odd – odd?" The whole place seemed to be full of his whispering.

"It's magnificent!" said Sandy, revelling in the strangeness of it. "See how those stones gleam? I wonder if they're valuable. And look at the shining streaks in that granite-like wall! I say, Tom, fancy –

perhaps we are the very first people to stand in this big underground hall!"

The underground river split into three in the big cavern. One lot of water went downwards into the steep tunnel, one wandered off to the other end of the cavern, and the third entered a smaller tunnel, and ran gently along it as far as Sandy could see.

"We'll follow this second one that goes to the other end of the cave," said Sandy. "We needn't wade in it — we can walk beside it. Come on."

So they walked beside it, and found that it wandered through a narrow archway into yet another cave — and there they saw a strange sight.

The water stopped there and formed a great underground lake, whose waters gleamed purple, green and blue by the light of the boys' torches. The lake was moved by quiet ripples. Tom and Sandy stood gazing at it.

"Isn't it marvellous?" whispered Tom, and again his whisper ran all round and came back to him in dozens of echoes.

Sandy suddenly got out the candle and lit it. The flame flickered violently and almost went out.

"The air's bad in this cave!" cried Sandy. "Come back to the other, where the rushing water is! Quick!"

He and Tom left the strange lake, and ran back to

the great, shining hall. The air felt much purer at once and the boys took big breaths of it. The candle now burned steadily.

"For some reason the air isn't good yonder," said Sandy. "Well, we can't go that way! There's only one way left – and that's to wade down that tunnel over there. Maybe it's the right one!"

"We'll hope so," said Tom, doing some more exercises, and jumping up and down. "Come on, Sandy. In we go!"

So into the water they went once more. How cold it was again! The tunnel was quite high above the water, and the stream itself was shallow, only up to their knees. It was quite easy to get along.

They waded along for a long way, their torches lighting up the tunnel. And then a very surprising thing happened.

They heard the murmur of voices! Tom and Sandy listened in amazement. Perhaps it was the noise of the stream? Or strange echoes?

They went on again and came out into a small cave through which the stream flowed quite placidly. And there they heard the voices again!

Then suddenly the voices stopped, and an even more peculiar sound came. It was the sound of somebody playing an organ!

10

A Very Strange Discovery

Sandy clutched hold of Tom, for the sound crept into every corner of the cave and filled it full. They were drowned in music!

It went on and on and then stopped. No further noise came, either of voices or music. The boys flashed their torches into each other's faces and looked at one another in amazement.

"An organ! In the heart of the mountain!" said Tom, in an amazed whisper. "Didn't it sound wonderful?"

"Come on – let's get out of this cave and see what's in the next one!" whispered Sandy. "Maybe there's an underground church here, with somebody playing the organ!"

The boys crept along, one behind the other. They suddenly saw a light shining through a rugged opening in the cave. It came from a cave beyond. Sandy peeped round to see what it was.

A lantern swung from a rope in the roof of a cave. It was a large cave, and in it were the two men who lived in the old cottage! They were crouched over the machinery that Sandy had seen in the back room!

Sandy clutched Tom's hand, and his heart leaped and beat fast. So they had actually come to the cave behind the gushing spring that fell from the hole in the rock!

They could hardly believe their good luck! They squeezed each other's hand, and wished that the men would go away from the machinery, whatever it was, so that they might see what it was.

"I wish they'd go back to the cottage," whispered Sandy, and at once his whisper ran round and round and sounded like a lot of snakes hissing! The men looked up in alarm.

"What was that noise?" said one.

The second man answered in a language that Sandy knew was German. He *wasn't* deaf and dumb then! Sandy rejoiced. They were spies, he felt quite sure. But how could he make them go away, so that he and Tom could examine the cave properly.

Sandy had an idea. He suddenly began to make the most dreadful moaning noises imaginable, like a dog in pain. He made Tom jump – but the two men jumped even more. They sprang up and looked round fearfully.

"Oooh, ah, ooh-ooh-ah, wee-oo, wee-oo, waaah!" wailed Sandy. The echoes sent the

groaning noise round and round the cave, gathering together and becoming louder and louder till the whole place was full of the wildest moaning and wailing you could imagine!

The men shouted something in fear. They ran to the stream, jumped into it, waded in the water till they got to the rock through which it flowed, and then wriggled out of the hole, down to the ground below, on the sunny hillside. They had never in their lives been so terrified.

Tom and Sandy screamed with laughter. They held on to one another, and laughed till they could laugh no more. And the echoes of their laughter ran all around them till it seemed as if the whole place must be full of laughing imps.

"Come on, let's have a look round now," said Sandy at last. They ran into the men's cave and then Tom saw what the "machinery" was!

"It's a radio transmitter!" he cried. "I've seen one before. These men can send out radio messages as well as receive them – and oh, Sandy, that's what they've been doing, the wretches! As soon as they see the steamers pass on the sea in the distance, they send a radio message to some submarine lurking near by, and the submarine torpedoes the steamers!"

"Oh! So that's why there have been so many steamers sunk round our coast," said Sandy, his eyes flashing in anger. "The hateful scoundrels! I'm going to smash their set, anyway!"

Before Tom could stop Sandy, the raging boy picked up a stone and smashed it into the centre of the transmitter. "You won't sink any more steamers!" he cried.

"Good," said Tom. "Now let's wriggle to the

hole where the stream gushes out, Sandy, and see if the men are anywhere near. If they're not, we could wriggle out, and go back to the girls over-ground. I really don't fancy going all the way back underground!"

"Nor do I," said Sandy. "It would be much quicker if we got out here, went up to the top of the mountain, and climbed down from there to where the girls are waiting."

"Fancy, Sandy — we've been right through the mountain!" said Tom. "I guess no boy has ever had such an adventure as we've had before!"

"Come on," said Sandy. "I'll go first."

He was soon at the mouth of the hole. He peered out but there was no one about at all, not even the big dog. "I bet the men have run into the cottage, taken the dog to guard them, and locked the door!" called back Sandy.

"Well, your wails and groans were enough to make anyone jump out of their skin!" said Tom. "I got an awful scare myself, Sandy!"

The two boys wriggled out of the hole, soaked again by the rushing water. But once they stood in the warm sun they forgot their shivers and danced for glee.

"Come on!" said Sandy. "No time to lose! The climb will make us as warm as can be!"

Off they went, climbing up the mountainside, revelling in the feel of the warm heather. The sun shone down and very soon they were as warm as toast — too warm, in fact, for Tom began to puff and pant like an engine!

They went over the top at last, sparing a moment to look back at the magnificent view. Far away they could see the blue sea, with a small steamer on it. "The submarine can't be told about you!" said Sandy. "Come on, Tom."

On they went. Tom followed Sandy, for Sandy knew every inch of the way. Down the other side they went, scrambling in their swimsuits over the heather. And presently in the distance, they saw the blue frocks of the two girls.

Sheila was bending anxiously over the pothole, wishing the boys would come back. It was so long now since they had gone down the hole. She almost fell down it herself when she heard Sandy's shout behind her.

"Hello! Here we are!"

The girls leaped to their feet and looked round in amazement. They were so surprised that they couldn't say a word. Then Jeanie spoke.

"How did you get out of the pothole?" she gasped. "Sheila and I have been sitting here for hours, watching — and now you suddenly appear!"

"It's a long story," said Sandy, "but a very surprising one. Listen!"

He sat down on the heather and he and Tom told how they had made their way through the heart of the mountain, wading and swimming in the river, and how they had found the strange underground lake, and had taken the right turning to the cave behind the spring. When they told about the men, and how Sandy had frightened them with his groans and wails, the girls flung themselves backwards and squealed with laughter.

"And now we know the secret of why our steamers on this coast are so easily sunk," finished Sandy. "It's because of those two traitors and their radio. Well, I smashed that! And now the best thing we can do is to go back home and get the police again!"

"What about our clothes?" asked Tom.

"They can wait," said Sandy. "We'll get them from the pothole sometime. We ought to go and get the police before the men discover that I've broken their radio, and escape!"

"Come on then!" cried the girls, jumping up, "We're ready!"

And down the hillside they all tore, the two boys in their swimsuits, with their oilskin bags still hanging round their necks!

11

The Hunt for the Two Spies

Miss Mitchell jumped in surprise when the four children rushed into the garden where she was busy cutting flowers — the boys in their swimsuits, and the girls squealing with excitement.

"Miss Mitchell! Miss Mitchell! We've found out all about the two spies!"

"Miss Mitchell! We've been down the pothole!"

"Miss Mitchell! We know how those steamers were sunk!"

"Miss Mitchell! Can we phone the police? Listen, do listen!"

So Miss Mitchell listened, and could hardly believe her ears when the children told her such an extraordinary tale.

"You dared to go down that pothole!" she gasped. "Oh, you naughty, plucky boys! Oh, I can't believe all this, I really can't."

Mrs MacLaren came home at that moment and the children streamed out to meet her, shouting their news. Mrs MacLaren went pale when she heard how Sandy and Tom had actually climbed down the dangerous pothole.

"Well, you certainly won't do *that* again!" she said firmly. "You might have killed yourselves!"

"But, Mother, our clothes are still down there," said Sandy. "We'll have to get them."

"You are far more important to me than your clothes," said Mrs MacLaren. "On no account are you to go pothole climbing again! And now – I think I must certainly ring up the police."

The children clustered round the phone while Mrs MacLaren rang the police station. They were so excited that they couldn't keep still!

"Do sit down," begged Miss Mitchell. "How can your mother phone when you are jigging about like grasshoppers!"

Mrs MacLaren told the sergeant what the children had discovered. When the sergeant heard that Sandy had smashed the spies' radio with a stone, he roared with laughter.

"Ah, he's a bonny lad, yon boy of yours!" he said into the phone. "He didn't wait for us to see if that radio was really doing bad work – he smashed it himself! Well, Mrs MacLaren, I'm fine and obliged to your children for doing such good work for us. This is a serious matter, and I must get on to our headquarters now, and take my orders.

I'll be along at Kidillin House in a wee while!"

Mrs MacLaren put the phone down and turned to tell the children. "Can we go with the police, Mother? Oh do let us!" begged Sandy. "After all, we did find out everything ourselves. And if those men have escaped, by any chance, we would have to show the police how to squeeze in through the rock where the spring gushes out."

"Very well," said Mrs MacLaren. "But go and put some clothes on quickly, and then come down and eat something. You must be very hungry after all these adventures."

"Well, so I am!" said Jeanie, in surprise. "But I was so excited that I didn't think of it till you spoke about it, Mother."

"I'm jolly hungry too, Aunt Jessie!" said Tom. "Come on, Sandy, let's put on shorts and jerseys, then we'll have time for something to eat before the police come."

The children expected to see only the constable and the sergeant – and they were immensely surprised when a large black car roared up the drive to Kidillin House, with six policemen inside!

"Good old police!" said Sheila, watching the men jump out of the car. "I love our London policemen, they're so tall and kind but these police look even taller and stronger! I guess they won't stand any nonsense from the spies!"

An inspector was with the police — a stern looking man, with the sharpest eyes Sandy had ever seen. He beckoned to Sandy and the boy went to him proudly.

"These spies may know they have been discovered, isn't that so?" asked the policeman. "They have only to go into their cave to see their radio smashed, and they would know that someone had guessed their secret."

"Yes, sir," said Sandy. "So I suggest that half your men go in the car to the other side of the mountain, and go up the slope there — it's a pretty rough road, but the car will do it all right — and the other half come with us up this side. Then if the spies try to escape the other way, they will be caught."

"Good idea," said the inspector. He gave some sharp orders, and three of the men got into the car and roared away again. When they came to the village of Kidillin, they would take the road that led round the foot of the mountain and would then go up the other side.

"Come on," said the inspector, and he and the children and two policemen went up the hillside. The dogs, of course, went too, madly excited. Sandy said he could quieten them at any moment, and to show that he could, he held up his finger and called "Quiet!" At once the two dogs stopped their yelping and lay down flat. The inspector nodded.

"All right," he said. "Come along."

They trooped up the mountainside. When they came fairly near the old cottage, the children had a great disappointment. The inspector forbade them to come any further!

"These men may be dangerous," he said. "You will stay here till I say you may move."

"But, please, sir," began Sandy.

"Obey orders!" said the inspector, in a sharp voice. The children stood where they were at once, and the three men went on. The dogs stood quietly by Sandy.

It seemed ages before the children heard anything more. Then they saw one of the policemen coming down the heather towards them.

"The men are gone!" he said. "Our men the other side didn't meet them, and we've seen no sign of them. Either they've escaped us, or they're hiding somewhere on the hill. They've left their dog though. We've captured it, and it's tied to a tree. Don't let your two go near it."

The children looked at one another in dismay

and disappointment. "So they've escaped after all!" said Tom. "Well, what about us showing you where the radio is? We might as well do that while we're here."

So the two boys took the six policemen to the hole in the rock, where the water gushed out. Two of the men squeezed through after Sandy and Tom, who once more got soaked! But they didn't care! Adventures like this didn't happen every day!

The men looked in amazement at the "machinery" in the cave. "What a wonderful set," said one of the policemen, who knew all about radios. "My word! No wonder we've had our steamers sunk here – these spies had only to watch them passing and send a radio message to the waiting submarine. We'll catch that submarine soon, or my name isn't Jock!"

"It's a strange sort of place, this," said the other policeman, looking round.

Sandy startled the policeman very much by suddenly clutching his arm and saying "Sh!"

"Don't do that!" said the man, scared. "What's up?"

"I heard something over yonder," said Sandy, pointing to the back of the cave. "I say – I believe the spies are hiding in the mountain itself! I'm sure I heard a voice back there!"

The policeman whistled. "Why didn't we think of that before! Come on, then — we'll hunt them out. Do you know the way?"

"Yes," said Sandy. "There's another cave behind this, and then a tunnel through which a shallow stream runs, and then a great underground hall, with an odd lake shining in a separate cavern."

"Good gracious!" said the policeman, staring at Sandy in surprise. "Well, come on, there's no time to lose."

They followed Sandy into the next cave. The boy lit the way with his torch. Then they all waded up the stream in the dark rocky tunnel and came out into the enormous underground hall. And at the other end of the great cavern they heard the sound of footfalls as the two spies groped about, using a torch that was almost finished.

"Give yourselves up!" shouted the first policeman, and his voice echoed round thunderously. The spies put out their light and ran, stumbling and scrambling, into the cave where the underground lake shone mysteriously. Sandy remembered that the air was bad there.

He told the policeman. They put on their own torches and groped their way to the cave of the lake. The air was so bad there that the two spies, after breathing it for a minute or two, had fallen to the ground, quite stupefied.

The policemen tied handkerchiefs round their mouths and noses, and ran in. In a moment they had dragged the two men out of the lake-cave and while they were still drowsy, had quickly handcuffed them. Now they could not escape!

Sandy and Tom were dancing about in excitement. The spies were caught! Their radio was smashed! Things were too marvellous for words!

It took them some time to squeeze out of the hole in the rock, with two handcuffed men, but at last they were all out. The surprise on the inspector's face outside was comical to see!

"They were in there, sir," said a policeman, jerking his head towards the caves. "My word, sir, you should see inside that mountain! It's a marvellous place."

But the inspector was more interested in the capture of the spies. Each of them was handcuffed to a policeman, and down the hill they all came, policemen, spies, children – and dogs! The big dog belonging to the men was taken over the hill by one policeman, to the car left on the road below. Mack and Paddy had barked that they would eat him up, and looked as if they would too!

"So the spy-dog had better go by car!" said the inspector, smiling for the first time.

12

The End of the Adventure

What an exciting evening the children had, telling their mother and Miss Mitchell all that had happened! Captain MacLaren came too, on twenty-four hour's leave, for the police had phoned him, and he felt he must go and hear what had happened.

"It's a great thing, you know, catching those two spies," he said. "It means we'll probably get the submarine out there that's been damaging our shipping – for we'll send out a false message, and ask it to get in a certain position to sink a ship but our aeroplanes will be there to sink the submarine instead!"

"Could we explore the inside of the mountain again, please, Uncle?" asked Tom.

"Not unless I am with you," said Captain MacLaren firmly. "I promise you that when I get any good leave, and can come home for two or three weeks, or when the war is over, we'll all go down there exploring together. But you must certainly not explore any more by yourselves. Also, the winter will soon be here, and the rains and snow will swell that underground lake, and the streams, and will fill the caves and tunnels almost to their roofs. It will be too dangerous."

"Uncle, when we do explore the heart of the mountain with you, we could find out if the river there is the beginning of the Spelter," said Tom, eagerly. "We could throw something into it there – and watch to see if what we throw in, comes out at the foot of the mountain where the river rushes!"

"We could," said Captain MacLaren, " and we will! We'll have a wonderful time together, and discover all kinds of strange things!"

"But we shall never have quite such an exciting time again, as we've had this last week or two," said Sandy. "I couldn't have done it without Tom. I'm jolly glad he and Sheila came to live with us!"

"So am I!" said Tom. "I'm proud of my Scottish cousins, Uncle Andy!"

"And I'm proud of my English nephew and niece!" said the captain, clapping Tom on the back. He looked at them with a twinkle in his eye. "I did hear that you couldn't bear one another at one time," he said, "and that you and the dogs were all fighting together!"

"Yes, that's true," said Sandy, going red. "But

we're all good friends now. Mack! You like old Paddy, don't you?"

Mack and Paddy were lying down side by side. At Sandy's words Mack sat up, cocked his ears, and then licked Paddy on the nose with his red tongue!

"There you are!" said Sandy, pleased. "That shows you what good friends they are! But I shan't lick Tom's nose to show he's my friend!"

Everybody laughed, and then Miss Mitchell spoke.

"I wonder what's happening to those two spies," she said. And at that very moment the telephone rang. It was the inspector, who had called up the captain to tell him the latest news.

"One of the men is a famous spy," he said. "We've had our eye on him for years, and he disappeared when war broke out. We are thankful to have caught him!"

"I should think so!" said the captain. "What a bit of luck! It's difficult to round up all these spies — they're so clever at disappearing!"

"Well, sir, they won't do any more disappearing — except into prison!" said the inspector, chuckling. "And now there's another bit of news, sir, I don't know if you've heard it?"

"I've heard nothing," said the captain. "What's the second piece of news, Inspector?"

"It's about that submarine, sir. We've spotted it and we've damaged it so that it couldn't sink itself properly."

"Good work!" cried the captain in joy. "That is a fine bit of news!"

"We've captured the submarine," went on the inspector, "and we've taken all the crew prisoners."

"What have you done with the submarine?" asked the captain, while all the children crowded round him in excitement, trying to guess all that was said at the other end of the telephone.

"The submarine is being towed to Port Riggy," said the inspector, "and if the children would like to come over and see it next week, we'll be very pleased to take them over it, to show them what they've helped to capture!"

"What does he say, what does he say?" cried Sandy. "Quick, tell us, Father!"

"Oh, he just wants to know if you'd like to go over to Port Riggy next week, and see the submarine you helped to capture!" said the captain, smiling round at the four eager faces.

"Who said we should never have such an exciting time as we've been having!" yelled Tom, dancing round like a clumsy bear. "Golly! Think of going over a submarine! Miss Mitchell – you'll have to give us a day's holiday next week, won't you?"

"Oh, it depends on how hard you work," said Miss Mitchell, with a wicked twinkle in her eye.

And my goodness, how hard those four children are working now! They couldn't possibly miss going over to Port Riggy to see that submarine, could they?